Malcolm Karma: Cold Turkey

Also by Neil Christiansen

Dark White

Malcolm Karma

Cold Turkey

Neil Christiansen

Weathered Press

Part One

Malcolm

Chapter One

There's blood on my sheets. A lot of it. For a moment I'm full of panic. What happened, where's... then the pain in my arm comes back and I remember. I let out a lungful of air and relax. It's okay, it's my blood.

There's no way it's coming out of the sheets, so they go in the trash, double bagged, along with the mattress pad too. After the bed is remade I pull on my slacks from the night before and head to the kitchen. There's strong coffee waiting for me on the stove. I fill a shallow ceramic mug and walk out the sliding glass door of my apartment to my tiny ground floor patio.

The wound on my arm burns. The bandage is soaked through and dried to a crusty rust color. It needs cleaning, but it can wait till after the coffee. It's my ritual, sipping java on plastic lawn furniture. Staring at the morning sun hovering over the lifeless retaining pond. It's the suburbs.

It's hard to feel more than two dimensional living in the burbs. They're flat and endless with no character or energy.

The parking lot of my building, packed with blue and gray sedans and minivans at six a.m. is virtually empty by seven. The residents parade out, single file, like it's some sort of national holiday celebrating mediocrity. At six in the evening they shuffle back in and you'd never know anything had happened.

It makes you feel small. It makes you feel invisible. That being said, sometimes in life it's not about how you feel. Sometimes it's just about knowing who you have to be and then making yourself be that. For example, when I wake up in the morning I don't feel like a killer, and yet...

The day is slow and long. A kind of tortured purgatory, like being drawn out on the rack for twelve hours. The boredom manifests as a physical pain, compounding the discomfort of my wounded arm. There's tightness in my chest and a knot in my shoulders. I don't like the person I am, but it's the only person I know how to be, and besides, I don't have much choice in the matter.

Still, I can't do it anymore. I need more from life. I need to feel human. I need— what I need is to be able to sleep at night without the nightmares. I need peace. So this is it. After tonight, I'm done. One way or the other. I'm through.

———

At eight p.m. the cool evening air begins to roll in, and with it come the clouds. I shower and shave. Vodka from the freezer goes into a rocks glass over two garlic stuffed olives. I set the glass on my dresser. Drinking helps me deal with the trauma, but it's a fine needle to thread. Too much, even a little too much and I'll be foggy and unreliable when I go to work.

My uniform is exactly what you'd expect. Black slacks,

white shirt, black tie and jacket. My hair is short and clean cut, parted neatly and free of product. I have a Beretta .45 in a hip holster under my jacket and a small four inch switchblade in my right pants pocket.

By nine o'clock the sun has dipped below the horizon and the moon is a washed out blotch of cream colored light halfway up the sky. The thunder started half an hour ago and now the rain is falling in huge aggressive drops. I'm soaked to the bone by the time I reach my car, and even with the wipers on full the windshield is a streaky watercolor of yellow and black.

When the engine of my twenty year old Cadillac starts up, the cassette in the deck clicks on and Johnny Cash announces that God's gonna cut me down. I nod my head in silent agreement and brush the wet hair back off my forehead. My reflection in the rearview mirror stares back at me with disdain and I wipe the palms of my hands across my face. They're rough and gritty even though they're wet. I grip the steering wheel at ten and two and inspect my worn out knuckles. It's about making yourself believe you are who you need to be. In my case, it's about remembering that I hate myself.

The open flesh on my arm burns and draws my focus. I'm damaged goods, broken and unwanted. Crimson from the wound seeps through the white fabric cuffs of my shirt and rain pounds the thin steel roof of the car while the hill billy on the radio shouts at me about God's wrath. Suddenly I slip into the person I'm looking for. The transformation feels oily and sick, like a fever about to break. Anger churns in my chest and tension tightens up the muscles in my back in anticipation of what is coming.

I drop the car into gear and feed gas to the engine. It growls and kicks and bucks, but I hold the wheel tight as it surges out of the parking lot and heads east towards the lights of the city.

————————————

I've put a lot of thought into it, and what I've come up with is this. I wish it was harder. It seems to me that killing a man should be difficult, and I wonder what it says about us, as people, that we've worked harder and harder to make it easier and easier. The time and resources that we've put into simplifying the act of taking another life... well, it isn't hard and it only takes a moment.

I park my car in a concrete tower a few blocks from my destination and walk in the drowning rain. The drive took time, and that anger I worked so hard to achieve at home has mellowed into a melancholy ache in my throat. I'm going to have to get that feeling back before I can do what needs doing.

When I get to his building I stand on the stoop and stare up at the flat brick face of it. He lives here, I assume. He has a sofa and a television, plates and bowls and probably breakfast cereal in a cardboard box. He thinks he's just a guy and tonight is just a night. I hate that it's me that has to prove him wrong.

A half a block further I walk into the alley between his building and the next. There's a quiet spot just inside the shadows where I crouch down and wait. The rain slows down and I watch it peter out to a sad little drizzle in the yellow glow of the street lamps. It isn't long after that.

The steps come slow and casual, splashing lightly across the wet cement with a patience I wish I felt. Then his profile breaks through the edge of my field of vision and for a moment he's perfect. A beautiful dark silhouette on the oil painting of my city. I want nothing more in that moment than for him to live. Moments like this are painfully short.

I step forward into the light and before he can turn his head, my switchblade snaps open like a thunderclap and the blade is between his ribs. He gasps and chokes and my left hand is around his throat, holding him up. I pull him in against me, like a lover, and whisper in his ear.

"Relax Chris, I promise this will be fast. I don't want to hurt you, at least not for long."

In two quick steps we turn and I throw him against the soft weathered brick of his home. His head bounces off it like a rubber ball and the confusion vanishes from his eyes as they roll up into his head. He collapses on the pavement in a crumpled mess of bloody laundry.

The candy apple red from his side mixes with the rainwater creating a cascade of pale pink liquid that pools at my feet. I think of the blood from my arm mixing with his, creating a symphony of DNA on the wet asphalt and feel profound indifference. A pat down of his pockets produces a crumpled pack of Marlboros and a lady's Zippo lighter.

I pull my gun and crouch across from him, watching the vanishing drizzle dance on his pale face. I light one of his cancer sticks and smoke while I wait for him to come back to me. Towards the end of the butt his eyes flutter and open with a desperate rattled expression.

I level the barrel of my weapon between his eyes.

"Hi Chris," I say.

He's bleeding a lot and not quite sure where he is. I know it hurts for him to breathe and the pain in his ribs is preventing him from sitting up.

"It's okay Chris," I say. "You don't have to sit. Just lie there for now. Try and stay comfortable."

He's frightened, obviously. Not sure what to make of

me. He breathes shallowly and winces when he tries to move. Eventually he takes my advice and settles into a position that seems to provide the least agony.

"I know it hurts," I say with compassion. "And I'm sorry for that. Believe it or not, I've been exactly where you are now. I really do know what you're going through."

I reach out and brush his hair out of his face. I hold his cheek in my palm and look him straight in the eyes.

"Chris, I don't want you to feel like you have to do a lot of talking tonight, okay? I know it's difficult so I'll try and keep the conversation centered around yes or no kinds of questions. Okay?"

He looks at me pitifully and I wish I could make it all better for him. This is not the mood I need to be in. After a moment he nods and I smile.

"Good job Chris. You got it perfect."

He coughs and his lips turn red. I put the cigarette out on the pavement and lean in a bit.

"We'll start simple," I say. "Do you know who I am Chris?"

His head shakes no.

"Of course not. There's no reason you should. Do you know why I'm here?"

There's a pause, then he coughs again and tries to speak.

"Money?" he wheezes.

I pout and shake my head.

"Oh Chris, no. No, it's not money."

I crouch and get very close to the ground. I turn my head and look him deep in his eyes. I want to see his reaction. I want to be there when he realizes.

"Do you know Kelly Phillips, Chris?"

His shallow breath stops and the pupils in his eyes go wide.

"Right," I say. "That's what I thought."

Sitting up again, a tense anger begins to churn in my stomach. It's coming back, moving through my muscles, spreading into my legs and chest, through my shoulders and neck and down my arms to the very tips of my fingers. It's exactly what I was looking for.

The man is trying to move now. His breath is back, but short and fast. His face is painted in earthy shades of panic. He's coughing and I can hear the blood in his lungs. He's trying to talk. He wants to explain. They always want to explain.

"I—"

I let out a long sigh.

"You what, Chris?"

Tears begin to pool at the corners of his eyes. His choking bloody breaths take on the telltale characteristics of crying.

"I didn't—"

"Yes you did Chris. You did. Right? I saw it in your eyes. Right now you wish you didn't, but you did."

He opens his mouth and his teeth and tongue are covered in blood.

"Can I tell you a secret Chris? I wish you hadn't too. I really do, and not just for Kelly's sake. I mean, that poor girl, she didn't deserve that. But no, I'm being selfish here. For me. I wish you hadn't for me. Every time I sit here like this I wish for it not to be the guy."

He looks at me like he's begging. Begging me to walk away. To let this be enough. To let it be over. It isn't though. That anger in my belly keeps getting hotter. Foggy rage keeps filling up my brain and clouding out my judgement.

"Just once," I say. "Just once I want her to get it wrong. For it to turn out that she has the wrong guy. Then I could actually sleep. I could go to Mica and say, *sorry you were wrong and I had to let him go.*"

He's outright sobbing now and blood is running down his chin and neck.

"I just want to be done with this Chris. I just want one excuse to tell her I won't do it anymore. But every time I have one of you pieces of shit like this, spitting blood and asking me to grant you mercy, every time, I mean every single time, you're guilty. How do I let you walk away when you did what she says you did?"

I stand up.

"How do I pretend that you didn't hurt that girl? How do I pretend that you won't do it again?"

He wheezes.

"I won't. I can't. I can't pretend Chris!"

I look down at him for a long time. He's crying and spitting and trying to crawl. After a minute I feel fatigue flood over me and I lift the gun and click the trigger without really thinking about it. There's a flash and the air shatters around us. I feel the detonation of the ammunition crash hard against my hand and the pressure wave moves through my arm and dissipates in my back.

When the ringing in my ears stops I'm sitting in my car. I light another of his cigarettes and crack the window an inch to let the smoke out, then drive home on auto pilot, not thinking about where I'm going, or where I've been. I sleepwalk into my apartment and stand in a hot shower until the water runs cold, then dry my hair in a soft warm towel and put a fresh bandage over the hole in my arm.

My gun and knife go in a safe in my closet and I slide

into a pair of thin cotton pajama pants. I climb silently into my cool crisp bed and lay my head on a firm memory foam pillow. The nightmares will be here soon, like they always are. My mind grows foggy and distant. As I drift towards sleep I feel my wife roll over and wrap herself around me.

Chapter Two

When I wake up my wife is in the shower singing to herself. I roll over and put my feet on the floor. I'm tired still and my body aches from the unused adrenaline produced last night. I cough up some brownish phlegm from the cigarettes and spit it in a tissue.

The shower stops and my wife walks in the room naked. She traipses over to her dresser with an energetic spring in her step.

"Good morning, love," she says, cheerfully.

"Good morning Elle," I yawn, while rubbing my eyes with both hands.

"How was work?"

I cough again.

"Long," I say.

"Tough client?"

"Not particularly. Pretty standard, just a late night."

She turns and looks at me sympathetically while she steps into her panties.

"Did you talk to Mica about cutting back on some of the night shifts?"

I yawn again, stretch and stand up.

"No, it was too late when I got done. I just wanted to get home. I thought I'd swing by this morning and have a few words with her."

"Well, be tough. Stand your ground. You've been doing all the over-nights lately. She's gotta have someone else that can take a night shift or two."

I laugh, walk over and kiss her forehead.

"I'll do what I can," I tell her.

I walk into the bathroom, grab my toothbrush and sit on the toilet, scrubbing my teeth while I do my business. Elle comes in, dressed now. She's in heels, stockings, and a skirt suit that's more than a little flattering on her. She spritzes her hair with some aerosol product and comes over to kiss me goodbye.

"What happened to your arm?" she asks, nodding at my bandage.

"Oh," I force a chuckle. "Scrapped it on the dumpster at work. Hey," I deflect. "How come everyone at work gets to see you all decked out in the naughty lawyer garb, but all I get is the jammy pants and t-shirt?"

She laughs. It's a nice laugh, easy and carefree.

"You got to see me naked two seconds ago."

"Not the same thing," I argue.

"Well, I'll tell you what. You go tell your boss to stop hogging all your evenings and I'll show you what a naughty lawyer I can be."

I smile.

"Deal," I say.

"Okay," she says. "Gotta go put away all those bad guys."

She kisses my lips and saunters out of the bathroom with a sassy sway in her hips intended to show me just what I'm missing when I work late.

I sigh. Time to put on my big boy undies and go talk to the boss.

Another shower, a new bandage, and I'm back in my uniform. I holster my weapon and comb back my hair. I'm out of the house by nine a.m. Steering my car back towards the city. Rehearsing my conversation in my head.

"Look Mica, I owed you. I owed you a lot, but that was fifteen years ago, and I've been working it off ever since. Don't you think we're even by now? Can't we just call it square?"

Even, ha! As if we could ever be even. How much is my life worth? If someone saves your life can you ever square that up? You're even when you get what was coming to you in the first place. No one is ever even with Mica Kole. No one ever gets to just walk away. You want out, she just takes back what she gave you in the first place. Your life.

The way I figure it, just broaching the subject has a better than even chance of being the last request I ever make. But I have to do it, because I can't go on this way. I'm scared of Mica, but I'm terrified of myself, of who I've become.

Not that I was a good person before. On the contrary, I was a big bag of shit and I didn't deserve the second chance she gave me. On paper Mica looks like the good guy, or ya know, gal as it were. She takes bad people, people like me, and either gets rid of them or puts them to good use. Good, I suppose, is a relative term. The point is, the legal system doesn't seem to be able to do its job, so I guess someone's gotta. If people knew what Mica was doing, they might just think she's a hero.

Hell, I used to.

———

Like I said, when I was nineteen I was a real piece of shit. The only reason I graduated high school is, failing me would have hurt the district's stats more than my future. I dealt pot and ecstasy and even a little heroin when I could get my hands on it.

I wasn't a good person, but I wasn't really a monster either. I was, well I was nothing. But I didn't know that yet. I wouldn't learn that little nugget until one unfortunate night in the city. See, I'd grown up in the suburbs, and all my rage and emptiness had been inflicted on other suburban kids. Kids who had soft lives and wealthy parents. Kids who were easy to take advantage of. Eventually I found out that the city is a much different place.

I had this client. I'm using that term loosely. Really he was just a kid I sold a bunch of E to. He comes to me one day and says he's got this cousin that's having a party and wants to buy a bunch of Molly.

"How much is a bunch?" I asked him.

"Like a ton! Like, maybe fifteen pills," he says.

Look, fifteen tablets of E is not a ton, but it was to this kid, and frankly it was to me too. It was enough that I didn't even have it to sell to him. I also wasn't going to pass up the money that it would bring in. Like I said, I was a piece of shit and I knew that I could dig up something that I could pass off as E. You give them a baggie with what you've got. Maybe six tabs. Then you back fill the rest with baby aspirin. At the sale you let them try a tab, but you make sure the good ones are on top, see. By the time the party is in full swing no one is going to say shit about the bad pills.

The nice thing about being a drug dealer, especially in the suburbs, is that there's no customer service department. No one's gonna come back and demand a refund.

"Well, I don't have that kind of quantity on me," I said. "But I'll put it together for you and let you know what it's gonna cost."

The kid looked at his feet.

"Actually man, she doesn't have any money."

I let out a grunt expressing my displeasure at him waisting my time.

"But she's really hot."

I gave him a bit of a grossed out face.

"Your cousin? You're telling me that your cousin is really hot? What the fuck is wrong with you?'

"Fuck off," he said, and turned aggressive. "She is. It's a fact. She's fucking hot as hell and she said she'd suck your cock for the pills. Not like you've never done that before."

"Yeah, for a pill, or a dime bag, or a little coke. Not for fifteen fucking doses."

The kid was pissed. Clearly he'd made promises. From the sound of it he'd received a few promises of his own. Fucking sicko.

"Look," I said. "Tell her it's all the way, and she brings a friend. Then I'll get her the pills."

He gave me a look like he was suddenly judging me for my perversity, but he nodded and said he'd let me know. The next day, we were on.

That weekend we drove to the city, a run down public housing complex on the north-side that locals knew by name. It was a concrete fortress of buildings, some abandoned, many with boarded up windows or burn marks on the cement. There was no security at the entrance or doorman to check in with. So we made our way to her place unannounced. When we rang the bell at her door it was opened by her old man.

He was middle aged and gnomish, in a greasy undershirt with his belly hanging out like he was eight and a half months pregnant. My client nodded at him and called him by his first name, then he pushed me through the door.

The walls in the place had once been white, but now resembled a grayish-yellow. There were smoke stains, uneven patterns of brown filth, across the ceiling. The carpet was worn down to threads and covered in crumbs and other disgusting debris.

We walked down a short hallway, past the kitchen, to a tiny bedroom with old Hello Kitty posters hanging loosely off the walls. My client introduced me to his cousin, then dropped himself on a twin bed lacking sheets or blankets.

The girls were cute, and clearly older than both of us. They started kissing each other before the door was even closed. After a minute of that they approached me and started reaching for my fly. That's when I put on the brakes.

"Whoa there honey," I said. "Not sure how your family works, but I'm not getting busy a room away from your old man, and I'm certainly not gonna pull out my dong in front of your pervy cousin here."

The girl shrugged.

"I thought this was the deal," she said.

"Yeah, sure. But don't you want to go someplace a little more private?"

She let out a frustrated groan.

"Do you even have the stuff?"

I pulled out a plastic zipper bag with three tabs of E and a dozen Aspirins that I had shaved down to match the real stuff.

"Alright then," she said. "We can go next door. Ain't no one using that hole for anything."

By next door she meant the next building over. The front door to the place was hanging on a single hinge and inside it was like standing in a filthy fireplace. Soot covered the walls and there were charred pieces of metal and glass strewn across the floor. In the corner of the entryway, maybe ten feet from the door was a thick dirty mattress.

I don't know what made me think that shagging in a burnt out condemned building was better than the previous alternative. I was pretty wound up at that point so, I suppose I just wasn't thinking at all.

The girls jumped on the mattress immediately and looked back at me while running their hands up under each other's shirts. My brain was on fire, and I had pins and needles running down my neck. I had tunnel vision looking at the two of them kissing and touching each other.

I walked over to the mattress and let them undo my pants. They pulled them down to my knees, then did the same with my boxers. The friend took my junk in her hand and squeezed it tight. I looked down at her to tell her to ease up and noticed that she wasn't even looking at me. The two of them were both starring right past me with matching grins.

Then I heard the click.

The two of them jumped up on the mattress and started laughing and squealing with overhyped girlish glee. They were bouncing and laughing and pointing, calling me profane names. I turned my head to see the father standing behind me with a dull, beat up looking revolver pointed right at my head.

They took the drugs, my wallet, my shoes and socks, my car keys and some pot I had on me for later, then the old man told the girls to get gone and they did. He ordered me to get on my knees. I did as I was told.

I started crying, kneeling there with my bare limp dick swinging between my pasty thighs, waiting for the sound I probably wouldn't even have time to hear. When the sound came though, it was different than I expected. Less of a bang and more of a crack. Then a loud grunt and a thud. After a moment of silence a new voice told me to get up.

The man standing behind me now was dressed like he was going to a funeral and holding a long wooden baseball bat. Next to him, on the ground, was the girl's dad, unconscious.

I was a blubbering mess. I tried to say thank you to the mystery man, but he told me I'd better not. Then he told me something that it would take me years to learn on my own.

"The day will come," he said. "When thanking me will be the last thing you want to do."

That's when he took me to meet Mica Kole.

Chapter Three

I park my car in a spacious parking lot on the Near Northside, not far from the CHA houses where all this began fifteen years ago. The neighborhood is very different now. It's upscale and expensive. I wonder for a moment what happened to that girl and her father. They certainly couldn't afford to live around here anymore.

Behind me is a wide, low, brown building with a red clay roof and a man-made brook that tumbles through dense coniferous vegetation. There's a small stone bridge that arcs over the water between the parking lot and the flat river-stone path that leads to the entrance.

The double doors at the front of the building are wide and fashioned out of two solid pieces of weathered lumber. They're thick and heavy, hung with black iron hardware. Inside, the lights are low and everything has a vaguely reddish glow. The space is divided into two large dining rooms, separated by a wide open-air kitchen. The tables are low to the ground and, absent chairs, surrounded by colorful overstuffed pillows.

I approach the host stand and tell the smiling young

Japanese girl to let Mica know that Malcolm Karma is here to see her. The girl smiles, bows politely, and disappears into one of the dining rooms. When she returns, she smiles again and tells me that Mica will see me.

On the other side of the dining room is a small doorway covered in a thick curtain of tiny multicolored beads. Outside the door stands an imposing man in a dark suit. Exactly the same suit I'm wearing. His name is Don, he's Mica's bodyguard. I don't know him well, and I'm thankful for that. He may not be the smartest guy, but he knows two things really well. One is that Mica is God, and the other is that everyone else is expendable. He nods at me as I pass through the curtain.

The room is uncomfortable. Small and a deep rusty red that plays tricks on the eyes. I've heard several guys have passed out in here from the vertigo it creates. Mica, as always, is sitting barefoot and cross legged on the floor behind a wide mahogany table. She smiles up at me as I remove my shoes and take a seat on a large forest green pillow across from her.

"Good morning Mal," she says, sweetly. "I had kinda thought I would see you last night. Everything go okay?"

I'm nervous. The gravity of what I'm about to do is hitting me and I can feel it pulling at my will to follow through. I clench my jaw and nod the affirmative to her.

"Yeah, it was just late," I say. "I wanted to try and catch Elle before she fell asleep."

"I see," she says.

There's an extended moment of silence, made longer by unbroken eye contact.

"Well," she says, finally looking away. "Here's your fee."

She lifts a wide business envelope off the table and

holds it out to me. I stare at it a moment before leaning forward and taking it out of her hand.

"Thanks."

She nods.

"So, I don't actually have anything for you today. I suppose that's a good thing, right?" she gives a light laugh. "But, ya know, I'll give you a call later this week when something comes up."

I sit paralyzed, unable to get up, but equally unable to say the words I've been practicing for days. There's sweat starting to work its way out of the pores on my forehead and the red walls are starting to inch in on me. The moment grows and quickly becomes uncomfortable as my frozen gaze drifts out of focus.

Mica tilts her head and squints at me questioningly.

"Everything went okay last night?" she asks again.

I nod silently, feeling my face drain of blood.

"Was there something you wanted to talk about?" she asks.

I feel a lump form in my throat and my hands go cold and clammy. My tongue dries up and stomach starts doing cartwheels.

"Mal, what's on your mind?"

I'm breathing too heavily and I start to get lightheaded.

"Mal, if you need—"

"I want out!" I blurt.

Mica stops and stares at me blankly.

"I— I know what you did for me. I— I know I owe you— owed you I mean. Uh. I just. Ya know, that was fifty— I mean fifteen years ago and I'm just— I'm not that kid anymore and uh—"

I'm spinning my wheels, trying to get traction on the

subject. I'm trying to be cool, but it's totally getting away from me.

"I love Elle. I— I want to have kids. I don't want—"

I feel like I'm going to throw up. I put my hands out on the table for balance.

"Malcolm!" Mica says, firmly.

The room is spinning. I lean forward and put my head on the table. Mica stands up and walks around to me. She kneels down and puts an arm around my shoulders.

"Slow down. Take it easy. Slow down, deep breath, it's okay Mal. Don't go passing out on me now."

My breath slows and the calm is coming back. Her delicate fingers are on my back rubbing soft circles, then up and down, caressing my neck with her fingernails. I take a long deep breath and begin to regain my composure. Suddenly, I'm very embarrassed.

"Mica, I—"

"Shh, I know it's hard," she says. "It's scary quitting your job for the first time. I know, I've been there too."

Her face is soft and friendly. She has deep emerald eyes that imbue a sense of trust. She pats me on the shoulder and smiles genuinely, then stands up and walks back around the table.

Behind her desk she crouches and lifts up an expertly hidden section of floor. In the hole her hands are busy and I hear the sound of two hollow clicks. A stack of manilla envelopes are visible for a moment before she pulls one out and the rest disappear back into the floor. When she's finished I can't even tell where the spot had been. She reaches out and offers me the packet.

"What's that?" I ask.

"Your retirement package."

I taste acid in my mouth.

"My what?"

"Like a pension," she says. "I set a little aside after every job, so when you're done you have something to get you going on your own."

I look at her dumbstruck.

"What did you think was going to happen Mal?"

I don't say anything.

She smiles again.

"Malcolm, you've done well. You've grown up. You're right, you're not the same person you were. The kid that came to me back then, he wouldn't even realize that what we do is wrong. You've become a good man and improved your character significantly. Hell, you worked for me and married a prosecutor. That takes a special kind of balls I'd say.

"You deserve to enjoy the rest of your life. Go, move out of town, make a baby and enjoy being unemployed for a while. I promise, we'll get by without you."

A huge sigh escapes my lungs and a thousand pounds of worry runs off my shoulders like dry sand. I smile and grip the envelope tightly.

"Thank you," I say.

Mica doesn't say anything, she just smiles and folds her arms across her chest.

I sand up and give a deferential bow.

"Thank you again."

I slip on my shoes and walk out the doorway. I'm only ten feet away when I hear Mica call Don into her office. As I walk out the front door I look back and see Don stepping in through the beaded curtain.

———

I drive home with a smile. The first envelope Mica gave me has nine hundred dollars in it. That's what I get, or I guess got, per job. Mica called it my fee, it's not really the right word. I didn't set the rate. I'm not, I wasn't, exactly an independent contractor.

That night in the city Mica's guy saved my life. That was it, I was owned. From then on Mica told me what to do, where to go, how to live, and how much I got paid. There was no negotiation. She bought my life by saving it, and I always figured I'd have to give it up to get it back.

I've never heard of anyone that quit, only those that disappeared. I assumed that you had to die to get out, so I'm more than a little surprised to find the second envelope contains a little less than seventy-five thousand dollars. A retirement payout from a job I thought I'd have to stop breathing to leave. I'm over the moon.

I stop at the florist on the way home and grab a dozen roses and baby's breath in a glass vase for Elle. A quick call to our favorite little French bistro and we're set with a reservation for nine o'clock.

At home I clean the apartment to perfection, even dusting the vertical blinds and scrubbing the outside of the fridge with Windex. I strip the sheets I just put on yesterday and replace them with our *Special Sheets*, then set candles around the room.

I put on nice clothes, ones with color in them, and make us cocktails in the fancy glassware we got at our wedding.

She walks in the door at eight p.m with a sour look on her face. I'm on the sofa watching the news on a comedy station. I hop up and grab her by both hands. She sighs and wiggles a bit to try and escape, but I hold on tight, crouching a little to get eye level with her, and flash her a big grin.

"What's wrong with you, grumpy pants?" I say, playfully.

She pulls her hands out of mine.

"Nothing, just a rough day at work," she says.

I turn and grab the flowers from the table next to us and hold them out to her.

"Maybe these will help."

She looks at them, then back at me with raised eyebrows.

"What did you do?"

I feign injury.

"What, a guy can't buy his sexy wife flowers without her accusing him of committing some kind of atrocity?"

She inspects the flowers with a skeptical eye.

"These are beautiful. So beautiful in fact, that if I had to guess, I'd say they coast at least a hundred bucks. So, I'll ask you again. Mal, what did you do?"

I grin.

"Oh boy," she says.

I dash to the kitchen and return with our drinks.

"So, I'm going to need a drink for this news?"

I smile and she takes the glass.

"Yes," I say. "For a toast."

"And to what are we toasting?"

My smile widens and I hold up my glass.

"I quit my job today."

Elle sets her drink down, hard, on the table. Gin splashes out over the rim and spreads across the surface.

"You did what?"

I nod my head.

"Yup, I went in and said that the job was interfering with our time together. That we were talking about starting a family and that I didn't see any way to make both work."

Well, ya know, close enough to the truth.

Elle stares at me with a look of, is that fear? Confusion? It feels like fear. Her face goes flush and there's a slight twitch in her eye. A moment later the color returns and a smile slowly creeps across her lips.

"For real?"

"For real, for real."

"And you want to start a family?"

There's a tremble in her voice that I can't quite identify. She takes a big sip of her drink and swallows hard, then throws her arms around me. We kiss, hard like we did when we were dating. I'm holding her face in my hands, her arms around my waist. She goes for my belt buckle and I grab her hands.

"We have dinner reservations," I say.

"I'm absolutely not hungry for food," she says.

I look her in the eyes and slowly let go of her hands. We hold eye contact and she undoes my belt, button, and fly. Her hands slide into my pants and she kisses me while her fingers start working. I start to grow and she pushes my pants off my waist.

"See," she says. "I told you I'd show you what a naughty lawyer looked like."

She lowers herself to her knees and takes me in her mouth. My hands run through her hair and down her neck and shoulders. My head leans back and I savor the intricate sensations made by her lips, and cheeks, and tongue.

I pull her up and kiss her mouth. My hands run down her back and up around her ass. I reach down and pull her pencil skirt up around her waist. My fingertips glide down her bare thighs to the tops of her stockings, then back up the inside to her panties. I push them aside and lift her up onto the table.

I stop kissing her and lift her chin with my fingers. I gaze into her deep brown eyes and tell her I love her, and I mean it more than anything I've ever said. I whisper that I need her. Slowly, as our breath gets shallow, I put myself close to her. She's not ready.

I lean back and look at her.

"We okay?" I ask.

She nods.

I lick my hand and use it to warm her up, then slide inside her. She lets out a long sigh and I pull close and kiss her again.

We make love on the table, in the bed, and again, clumsily, in the shower. When we're done at last, we lay sprawled out naked on the sofa. My fingers trace heart shapes on her bare tummy.

"We missed dinner," I tell her.

"Yeah, we did," she says. "But we had lots of dessert."

I smile at the corny joke.

"Are you hungry?"

"No," she says. "But I could use a cigarette."

"Well, I'll take that as a compliment."

"Take a walk with me," she asks.

"Gladly."

We grab the box of Camels and the lighter from the drawer in the kitchen. Elle throws on some sweats, and we head out the back to walk around the pond and smoke.

"So, what was rough at work today?"

"Oh, it's just frustrating. I had a witness for my case die. He was killed, actually. It looks like the suspect had it done and it means we may have to drop the charges."

"Wow," I say, surprised. "I didn't think things like that happened out here in the burbs."

She chuckles.

"Thankfully they usually don't. He was in the city last night and it looks like the suspect's gang took him out."

I stop walking.

"Last night?" I say.

"Yeah," she sighs. "He was out there tutoring some kid on the Northside and got jumped on the way back to his car. Stabbed and shot in the head."

I feel my throat close up and I start sweating.

"What was the case?"

"Oh, sad one," she says. "Young woman, a wife and mother. She was beaten pretty badly in a home invasion. Police think it was a robbery gone bad. Husband comes home in the middle of it and manages to chase the guys off, but the woman is in a coma, in critical condition.

"Husband was able to pick two of the guys out in a photo lineup though. He was set to testify, but now we're back to having nothing."

I feel tears forming in the corners of my eyes. I choke on my words.

"I think I — uh— I think I read about that one. What's her name again."

My wife looks at me with sweet concern.

"Yeah, you might have. It was in the papers a lot, about a month ago. Girl's name was Kelly Phillips."

My world comes crashing down around me. I picture the man lying on the wet pavement. I see his terrified eyes light up when I mention her name. I feel myself pull the trigger and smell the acrid sulfur scent of the gunfire mixing with the copper oder of the blood as it pools on the ground. I bend over and throw up on my shoes.

"Oh my God, honey are you—"

There's a clap of thunder and the sudden roar of rain, but the skies are clear and dry. I look up and see red. My nausea turns to panic and my eyes go wide. Elle turns, following my gaze and we stare together as our apartment building is consumed in flames.

Chapter Four

Elle screamed for a little, cried a bit longer and now she's sleeping in the grass with her head in my lap. The blaze burned for two hours while the fire department doused it with hoses and carried people out while wearing huge plastic masks that made them look like oversized insects. Now it's steaming in the moonlight, as the last of the engines turn off their spinning red lights and quietly roll away from the carnage.

As far as I can tell, no one died. Everyone lost everything, but no one lost their life. I find some consolation in that, even if it's only that it means the investigation will be less thorough. The police and fire marshal are still going through the wreckage though. Long heavy flashlights throwing harsh narrow beams of impossibly white light in the distance. Many residents have already been taken to the hospital for examination. Most of the others have left for hotels or to stay with family or friends. I've been letting Elle get some sleep, but it's getting late and I think it's time to get going.

I shake her gently and brush the hair from her eyes. She

opens them slowly, getting her bearings, remembering where she is.

"Fuck," she says.

"Yeah, it's for real."

We get up and I walk her to my car. I put her in the passenger seat and grab the spare key from the magnetic box under the rear wheel well. As I walk around to the driver's side I notice a tired looking man in a cheap, wrinkled suit approaching us from the remains of the building. I stop at the driver's door and watch as he walks up.

"You folks takin' off?" he asks, before he reaches me.

I nod a tired answer and gesture towards the car.

"I gotta get my wife to bed. She's pretty shaken up," I say.

"Sure, sure. I'm detective Upton."

He puts out his hand for me to shake. I take it an oblige.

"Malcolm," I say. "Malcolm Karma."

"Karma?" he says surprised. "Any relation to—"

"A.S.A. Elle Karma, yeah. She's my wife."

He nods and smiles.

"Well, very nice to meet you Malcolm."

"Likewise," I say, in my most exhausted tone.

He smiles again and gives me a once over, then sighs and gives a little shrug.

"Well, I won't keep you Malcolm. We're just trying to get a record of where everyone will be for the next day or so. Just in case we have to get in touch."

I nod understandingly.

"Right. Uh, we'll be at the motor lodge on Roosevelt Road."

He scratches the information in a small, squarish, black notebook. Halfway through he pauses and looks up a little confused.

"The motel you mean?"

"Yeah."

"I'm sorry, I don't have a polite way of asking this, so I'm just going to say it. Why?"

"Well," I say, with a slight edge of condescension. "I guess mostly because my apartment building is— well, was on fire."

He looks up from his notebook.

"Right," he says. "But why some fleabag motel? There's like a dozen decent hotels within five minutes of this place."

"Their sign says they have color TV," I say.

He doesn't seem to think this is funny.

"Look Detective, I don't want to be rude or difficult, but I don't see how the place we stay in is, frankly, any of your business. It's late and I really have to get my wife to bed, so unless there's something else..."

He's trying to mask his annoyance. Clearly he's not used to people talking to him this way, but after a moment he shakes it off and smiles back at me.

"Of course. I'm very sorry. I was just curious. Call it a professional habit. It doesn't matter at all. Just one more quick thing then. I just need your apartment number. Ya know, so we can make sure any personal items that may have survived get returned to you."

I look past him at the charred remains of our building and try to imagine a scenario where anything in the whole place survived intact. I look back at him and rub my eyes with my palms in exhaustion.

"Uh, one-oh-six," I say. "It's around back. Was. Was around back."

"Got it. Thanks so much Mr. Karma. We'll be in touch if we find anything out."

"Great," I say.

I climb into the driver's seat of my car and turn the engine over, drop the gearbox into second, feed it gas and pop the clutch. I let the tires squeal before gunning it out of the parking lot. It's true what I said about the motor lodge. They do have color TV, but that's not why we're staying there. Someone just burnt down my home and no part of me thinks it was an accident.

I quit my job with Mica Kole and despite her kind words and the lump of cash that I, thankfully, left in the car this afternoon, I know that this was, at best, a warning. More likely, it was intended to be my real retirement package. With any luck Human Resources thinks they did their job and isn't looking any further, but I'm certainly not going to risk running my credit card at the fucking Holiday Inn. A cash room at an unlisted motel is what this night calls for. I need to get Elle some sleep and help her clam down. Tomorrow I'll start figuring out what comes next.

I have to deal with the fire, but also, I have to look into the Kelly Phillips situation. Both of these mean dealing with Mica, and now that's going to be much, much more complicated.

Chapter Five

At six a.m. I climb out of bed without having slept. Elle is still comatose and I figure I'll let her sleep as long as I can. I put on my slacks and slide my bare feet into my loafers. After I pull my white undershirt on over my chest, I head outside.

The morning sun is still low over the city due east, down Roosevelt Road. It's a straight, uninterrupted ribbon of asphalt almost all the way to the lake. Traffic is light, but steady. The square parking lot that sits in the center of the U-shaped motel, however, is silent. I stretch and yawn, and walk across the gravely pavement to the manager's office. I need to get some coffee.

The lobby is old and musty. It looks as though it hasn't been renovated since 1973. Long, gold shag carpet is wearing thin in the high traffic areas. The formerly clear glass coffee pitcher is now only a shade or two lighter than its contents. Next to the pot is a stack of small white Styrofoam cups, and a couple of crusty bowls of sugar and powdered creamer.

I fill a cup with coffee barely dark enough to hide the

bottom of the cup and gulp it down. It's weak and bitter, as though it's been sitting in the pot for days, but I refill the cup and head back across the lot.

In my absence a couple of ladies have set up a small breakfast table in front of the room next to mine. They look young. Late twenties or early thirties, but they are wearing old flannel night gowns that look like they might have been stolen from my grandmother's closet. They have a rickety TV dinner stand between them and they're sitting on collapsible card table chairs. There's a tall thermos steaming into the crisp morning air on the table and two small paper plates holding toaster waffles and plastic silverware. They smile warmly as I approach.

"Good morning handsome," one of them says, in a thick and friendly Texas accent.

I smile back at the sound of her voice.

"Good morning ladies."

"You move in last night?" the other one says, in a slightly subtler accent of the same origin.

I glance at my door.

"Move in? God, I hope not, but yeah, got in last night. My apartment burned down so I needed a quick place to stay."

"Oh shit! That's what all that commotion was? I'm so sorry. Do they know what caused it?" the first one says.

"Not yet. Still investigating."

"Well, welcome to the off ramp to hell," she goes on. "Satan doesn't actually live here, but his place is walking distance."

I laugh.

"I'm Erica," she says. "This is my—"

She tilts her head a bit as if inspecting me, trying to determine what kind of man I am.

"My friend, Robin."

I smile and nod that I understand.

"It's very nice to meet you ladies."

"The pleasure is undoubtedly all ours," Robin says. "Now, why don't you dump out that swill they pass off as coffee in there and pour yourself a real cuppa Joe."

I raise my eyebrows and turn my cup over. Erica refills it with coffee from their Thermos. It smells rich and nutty and has a deep mahogany color that seems incongruous with the cheap cup it's swirling around in. I take a long sip and sigh with contented satisfaction.

"That is good coffee," I say.

Robin smiles.

"Only the best here," she says, with a twinge of irony.

"So, how long have you ladies been here at the Ritz?"

They look at each other and say in unison, "about three months."

I choke on my coffee.

"Three months? In this place?"

Erica laughs and nods her head.

"It's actually not that bad. It has a kind of low-rent romance to it."

I look around the rundown lot at the rows of brown steel doors wedged unevenly between the off white cinder-block walls. I suppose I can see what she's saying.

"So, what brings you ladies up here?" I ask.

Robin leans back in her chair and crosses her legs.

"Well, we're bounty hunters of a sort," she says, with a glib satisfaction that gives me the impression this usually knocks people right over. I have to admit, it does take me by surprise.

"Really?" I say, with just the right amount of awe.

"That's right."

"So, you're way up here chasin' bail jumpers?"

"Well, we're not so much that kind of bounty hunter," Robin says. "We don't do bail bond stuff no more."

"Well, we would," Erica cuts in. "But it doesn't pay what it's worth."

"Exactly," Robin agrees. "Plus, despite what they show on TV, it's actually pretty boring. We like a bit more excitement."

"Sure do," Erica says, with a gleam in her eye.

"That's fascinating. So what kind of bounty do you hunt then?"

"Well, right now we're contracting with a private organization. I guess you might say we're acting as debt collectors."

"I see."

The door to my room opens and Elle steps out looking like she's just gone ten rounds. I smile at her and give a wave.

"Good morning, sunshine," I say. "You look like you could use a cup of coffee."

I walk over and put my cup in her hands.

"I was just talking with our neighbors. Ladies, this is my wife Elle. Sweetheart, this is Robin and Erica. They are fascinating women, and Robin makes fantastic cup of coffee."

"Very nice to meet you," Elle manages.

We make a few more pleasantries and refill our coffee from Robin's Thermos, then we excuse ourselves to our room for Elle to get cleaned up.

"Obviously I'm not going into work today," she says.

"I figured as much, but we're gonna need some stuff. Everything was in the apartment."

I hand her the envelope with nine-hundred dollars in it.

"Go get some clothes, some supplies, and some food. Use my car. I'll get a cab and go to the dealership to get new keys for your car and stop at the insurance agent to file a claim."

She agrees. We clean up and she heads out for her chores. I use the phone in the room to call a cab. I do need to take care of the items I listed to Elle, but first I need supplies, and the first item on that list is a gun.

The city is really two very different places. To the north lie the gleaming towers of glass and ivory shades of concrete. To the south are rows of hollowed out shells the city doesn't bother supporting. It's a class thing. It's a race thing. Push poor people and minorities out of sight and then just forget about them. It's not surprising, but it's disgusting.

Crime exists in both places, obviously, but on the South Side it's unapologetic. Theft, intimidation, and assault occur in broad daylight without the fear of interference by the police.

Come to think of it, I guess it's not that different.

Citizens skitter about, doing their best not to notice what is happening around them, or at least not to let anyone know they've noticed. Living in a place like this is hard. You have to keep your head down and do your best not to stand out.

On the other hand, those very things make this the place to come when you have errands like mine. The cab drops me off six blocks from where I want to be, but it doesn't surprise me that he won't go any further. I pay the fare and give the driver a nice tip for getting me as close as he did.

I left most of the money from my retirement package in the envelope back at the motel. Still, I brought enough to take care of what I need. That means I'm walking six blocks through the dusty backstreets of the South Side with a grand in my back pocket and no gun.

I'm walking east on 63rd Street, watching the neighborhood deteriorate around me like a time-lapse of the Armageddon. Folks on the street, sidewalks, and porches stare at me. Some shout behavioral instructions that are suggestive of self love. After about twenty minutes of this I finally reach my destination.

Southerby's Law Office is a piecemeal brick and cement-block box with a few passing attempts at architectural flourish that do little to distinguish it from, say, an Afghan prison. It stands alone on an empty block, a bare dirt parking lot to its left and overgrown grass to the right. The second floor has a large picture window cutout that's been sealed up with four narrow mismatched windows. The first floor has two doors that appear to be competing for the title of last door you'd ever want to step through. I smile to myself because I know it doesn't matter which door you choose. They both lead to the same stripped out, bare beams room that serves as the law office of Alex K. Pilsen.

Alex is a private lawyer that provides legal services at little or no cost to the disenfranchised poor of the city. He named his practice Southerby's to make it sound more elite in court. He's good, very good in fact, and he wins a lot. Partly because he knows the law cold, and knows how to work the system, but mostly because he has a reputation. A reputation for helping innocent people. It's almost ironic.

Most defense attorneys, especially those on this side of town, have a rule about not asking their clients if they're guilty or not. Alex not only asks, he investigates, and he investigates hard. If you show up in court with Alex Pilsen as your counsel it's because he believes you're innocent, and if he believes it, then chances are good the court will too.

The stories say that when Alex shows up for a meeting with the State's Attorney, the S.A. rethinks the charges. More often than not charges are dropped or drastically reduced before any of his cases make it in front of a jury.

There are other stories too. Whispered ones. Low voices in the front seats of cars parked in empty lots late at night. Those stories say that Alex plays both sides. If you're innocent he'll get you off, but if you're guilty, you're better off taking a plea because if you walk, Alex will help make sure you get what's coming to you.

They say he got started in the law when a vigilante named Gavin Gayle bailed him out of a tough spot. After that, Alex became a lawyer to help the innocent, but continued to use his previous underworld contacts to provide information to Gavin.

That was twenty years ago though, and Gavin Gayle is just an old urban legend. Mica Kole is the Angel of Death for baddies in this city. She's probably where those stories come from in the first place, and Alex Pilsen is a strait laced upstanding lawyer that I just happen to know can get me a gun.

I cross the street and approach the building. There are three tough guys in their late teens loitering outside. They see me walking over and take notice. The older one stands up and meets me at the curb.

"Keep walking Ringo," he says.

I raise my eyebrows and put my hands in my pockets to make myself less threatening.

"It's okay buddy," I say. "I'm here to see Alex. I'm an old friend."

That's probably pushing it. I'm not really anyone's friend, and I'm sure Alex wouldn't classify me that way if he were asked. Truth is, I'm just hoping that he's more committed to justice than he is to Mica, and that he gives me enough time to explain the difference before he has these kids turn me inside out.

"You don't look like no one's friend," one of the teenagers says.

"Actually, you look like a cop," another one adds.

I chuckle a bit.

"How's that funny?" the leader of the group says.

"Look, kids, I—"

I take a right hook to my jaw and it drops me to one knee. The little ones jump on me throwing punches to my ribs, kidneys and liver. They're persistent but weak, and as soon as I shake off the ringing in my head from the sucker punch I grab one of them by the hand and give a quick twist. His wrist breaks and he rolls off me screaming and crying.

The other one jumps off me and scuttles back a dozen feet or so. I take a quick step in his direction and he jumps back further.

I turn back towards the leader of the trio and say again, "I'm here to see Alex."

I wipe my cheek where he hit me and see blood soak into the cuff of my shirt.

The kid comes at me fast and sloppy. I step back and grab him by his right wrist with both hands. I two step around him and pull his arm up behind his back. I give it a jerk and feel the ball joint pull out of his shoulder socket, a trick Mica taught me when I first started working for her. I press my right hand hard on the injury and he drops to his knees with a scream.

"Thanks fella," I say.

The two wounded boys roll on the dirty asphalt street, moaning and grabbing at their injuries. The third kid is running away from the scene as fast as his overpriced sneakers will let him. I leave the two delinquents on the street and walk through the door on the right.

Alex looks surprised to see me. Surprised may be an understatement. He looks like he's seeing a ghost, but he recovers quickly and gives me a plastic smile that morphs into something more genuine.

"Mal, what a surprise," he says, honestly.

"I'm sure," I say.

"I just mean, Mica didn't say you were coming by today."

I laugh.

"I imagine Mica said I wouldn't be by at all anymore."

"I don't follow," he says.

"I'm retired."

Alex just about chokes on his coffee.

"Retired? Wow, well good for you."

"Yeah, sure. Mica was very gracious about it, until she had my apartment building burned down."

Alex's face goes flush for a moment. This whole visit is clearly rattling him.

"Have you talked to her lately?" I ask.

"A little bit this morning," he says.

I nod and look around his room casually. I begin wandering the space aimlessly.

"She didn't say anything about me?"

He shakes his head.

"No, not that I recall."

"Alex," I say, with a condescending tone. "You're a lawyer, you don't forget things."

He shrugs like he's looking for words.

"I'll get down to it," I say. "I asked Mica to get out. She said it was no big deal. She gave me a retirement payment and said to enjoy myself, then I go home and someone blows up my place and burns it to the ground."

"Mal—" he's trying to be professional now. "I'm sorry for your loss, but I couldn't sell that in court. That sounds like a coincidence. I don't see anything suggesting that it was Mica that set the fire."

I tilt my head and give him a glare.

"I also found out last night that the job I did the night before, my last job, it was a mistake. The client wasn't the right person. In fact, he was a witness for the prosecution in the case. He was due to testify in court yesterday."

He frowns and I can't tell if it's a put on or if he's genuinely surprised.

"Here's my problem," I say. "I've know Mica a long time."

Alex nods.

"Me too Mal."

"I know, and what I'm saying is that she doesn't make mistakes. I've never known her to fuck something up. She's—"

"Meticulous," Alex finishes.

I give a melancholy smile.

"Meticulous. That's right. She's meticulous."

"So, you're saying—"

"So I'm saying that, if you can spare one, I could really use a gun."

Alex stares at me for a long moment. He's thinking about what I've said and about what I've asked. He's trying to decide. He's playing a fast game of truth or consequences with himself. I stare back silently. There's nothing more for me to add. He understands what I'm asking and he understands why. I can't tell if he believes it, but I'm pretty sure he knows that I do.

He walks away from his desk and kneels down next to a tall stack of overstuffed file folders on the floor. He pushes them aside and lifts a section of floor boards. It crosses my mind that the apple doesn't fall far from the tree.

"What'd you guys get a Groupon or something?"

He looks back at me confused.

"Never mind," I say. "Guess you had to be there."

When he returns to his desk he has an oily looking black handgun with a slide, and a barrel like a large mouth bass.

"It's a .45," he says. "I don't have any ammo, you'll have to get that someplace else."

I nod in understanding.

"Don't come back here," he says.

"I won't," I assure him. "Maybe don't mention that I was here," I counter.

"I most assuredly will not," he says.

"You're gonna need new thugs out front," I say, as an afterthought while I'm walking to the door.

Alex chuckles.

"Those fuckers don't work for me," he says. "They only think they do."

I grab the door and swing it open.

"Mal," Alex calls as I'm stepping out.

I turn and look him in the eyes.

"You're living up to your name," he says, without a hint of humor.

I give a knowing nod.

"Watch yourself," he says. "This shit is bad karma."

I leave his door open as I cross the deserted street and head back to civilization.

Chapter Six

Once I'm out of the city's demilitarized zone I start looking for somewhere to get new clothes. I'm still wearing my digs from the night before. They're wrinkled and they smell like a house fire. I need something clean and a little formal, because my next stop is the restaurant to see Mica.

I find a thrift store buried inside the first neighborhood I pass through. I'm able to put together some dark blue jeans with a black collared shirt. A herringbone tweed jacket with black suede patches on the elbows is also a good find. I pay the girl at the counter in cash and change in the store's dressing rooms. On my way out I buy a used brown leather satchel and stuff the dirty clothes inside.

Moving back towards the highway I find a gun shop. I need bullets, so I stop inside and purchase a blue and white box of .45 rounds and a shoulder holster that'll fit the gun currently tucked in my waistband. Outside I put the holster under my jacket, load the pistol, and stuff the rest of the ammo in the briefcase. Forty minutes later I'm stepping out of the back of a black Lincoln Town Car in front of Mica

Scotti Sushi. I smile, she doesn't cook her fish, just her employees.

I walk in and make eye contact with the hostess. She smiles, unalarmed to see me, and I stroll past her into the part of the dining room farthest from Mica's office. I saunter up to the empty bar and find a seat.

"Morning partner," the bartender says casually as she empties a rack of glassware onto the shelves behind the bar.

"Too early for a drink?" I ask.

"No such thing my friend."

I smile.

"Great," I sigh. "Gin and tonic please. Double pour, Seagrams, with two lime wedges."

"A man who knows what he wants," she answers.

"I'm getting there."

"I'm Sarah."

"Nice to meet you Sarah. I'm Malcolm."

"Yes you are," she says.

She looks over for a moment, past the entrance, then back at her work. I resist the urge to glance over and see what she's looking at. My drink is placed in front of me just as a looming presence appears at the stool to my left.

"On the house," Sarah says, and disappears through a set of saloon doors to the back room.

I feel a heavy hand on my shoulder and the deep gravely voice of a Teddy Bear with teeth says my name.

I don't look up, but sip my drink and say, "Don."

The hand on my shoulder gives an unsubtle squeeze.

"What are you doing here Mal?"

I take another sip, swallow and give a refreshed sigh.

"I'm having a drink. Can I get you one?"

"Malcolm—"

"Oh, or did you mean what am I doing here, like, on this

plane of existence? Like what am I doing alive after you and your boss went through all that trouble to make me, well, not?"

Don uses the hand on my shoulder to turn me ninety degrees on my stool so that I'm facing him. I reach for my drink, but he grabs it first and upends it on the bar.

The hand on my shoulder gets a little tighter and I give an involuntary groan.

"You shouldn't be here."

"Well, I need to see Mica."

"You know that isn't going to happen," he says, with a slight tinge of sympathy in his voice.

"Actually," I say. "I think I'm going to see her whether I want to or not."

He frowns at me.

A cheerful but assertive voice breezes through the empty room.

"It's okay Don, I've got this."

We both look sideways and see Mica in a delicate cream colored sundress cut well above the knees pattering barefoot through the restaurant towards us.

Don looks at her with eyes that ask if she's sure about that. She waves him off casually. He glares at me and releases my shoulder before sulking away to the same back room the bartender disappeared into.

Mica steps up to the bar and smiles a bright sunny smile that betrays no surprise or displeasure. She hops up on the stool next to me and crosses her legs, leaning casually with one elbow on the bar.

"How's the drink?" she says, with the friendly tone of a proprietor chatting with a customer.

"Free always tastes good," I say.

She just stares at me with the same charming smile.

"It was just well gin," I say. "Fine for what it was."

"You could have ordered better."

"I didn't know that I wasn't paying for it when I ordered. I'm on a fixed income at the moment."

Her expression doesn't change.

"What are you doing here Mal?"

I sigh.

"Well, I thought maybe we should have a little chat."

"I didn't think we had anything left to say to each other."

"Ya know, I didn't either, but then I got homeless and thought maybe there were still some things to cover."

Finally she looks serious.

"What do you suppose that has to do with me?"

"Well, that's what I was hoping to find out."

She sits up straight and crosses her legs the other way.

"Mal, you shouldn't be here."

"What's going on Mica? Why don't I have a place to live? And what's the deal with the Phillips case? The guy didn't do anything, he was the primary witness for Christ's sake. Since when do we client witnesses? When did we stop being the good guys?"

Mica's face goes pale and earnest.

"Mal, you need to go. You need to leave, go home, and never ever come back here. I gave you your out. I did my level best for you, but we're done now. There's nothing else I can do for you. Go home. Go now!"

"Jesus Mica," I shout. "You aren't listening. I don't have a fucking home. You fucking burnt it down. What the hell happened? I knew we weren't good, but at least I thought we were on the good side. Or was it all a lie? Were we ever trying to do right?"

Mica is calm, even tempered, but stern and resolute.

"Malcolm, there is no we. There is just you, and this is me telling you to get out of this restaurant now and go far away. Far away and never come back."

We stare at each other for a long moment, then I feel that familiar hand on my shoulder.

"You had your shot Mica," I say. "You fucked it up and now I know you're coming. You won't get another chance. If I were you I'd think about letting it go."

"Funny," she says. "That's exactly what I was going to say to you. Let it go, Mal. Just fucking let it go."

I finish the rest of my chores: filing the insurance claim on our burnt down apartment and contacting our bank and credit card companies to get replacement cards. I stop by the BMW dealership to order a new set of keys for Elle's car. Then, before I go back to the motel, I swing by the old apartment.

The place looks like it belongs on the same block as Alex Pilsen's law office. It's charred and hollowed out, the ash a grayish mud, mixed with the water from the fire department's hoses. I sit there on the curb in front of the building for a good half hour taking it all in. Part of me just wants to see how it makes me feel. What does it do to me, looking at the carnage? But mostly I'm just waiting to see if there are any cops or fire investigators lurking around. After half an hour of waiting I decide it's clear and head in.

I step through the empty hole that was the building's front door and make my way down the devastated hallway to the back of the building where our apartment was. The steel door is still upright, but the frame stands alone, unsupported by the adjacent walls. I walk around it and stand for a moment in what was our living/dining room. The damage here seems even more intense. Any surface that remains is the Platonic ideal of black. Any trace of furniture has been reduced to soft ashen mud. It smells like campfire and battery acid and I gag a little as I walk through the ashy mud.

Past the kitchen I find the place in the wall that held my safe. The wall and all its supports are gone and the safe is lying face down in a pile of rubble and debris. It's heavy, but I manage to upright it and dial in the combination. The front pops open effortlessly and I find the contents to be more or less undisturbed.

I load the gun, knife, and a straight razor into my new bag along with a stack of cash wrapped in Saran Wrap. The plastic has melted to the outside bills, but the rest are fine. There's a small stack of various kinds of identification with my photo but different names. Useless now, melted into a solid block. I don't need them, but I don't want to leave them for someone to find and question down the road. There's a ring of six keys that I pocket in my jeans and a thick yellow paper envelope stuffed with color photographs that I tuck away in my jacket breast pocket.

I close the safe and tip it back over. A little dust on the top from some of the surrounding debris make it appear as it had when I arrived. I backtrack out of the building the way I came in and pull my phone out to order an Uber.

As I step out onto the black tar asphalt parking lot I hear my name. Startled, I turn around and see Detective Upton walking towards me. He's wearing the same suit he had on last night, and not looking like he's slept a wink since then either.

"It is Malcolm, right? Elle Karma's husband?"

I smile and try to force the surprise off my face.

"Oh, hi. Yeah, it's Malcolm, but ya know, Mal is fine. My friends call me Mal."

He smiles at me with piercing eyes that feel to me as though they are seeing inside me without my permission.

"I'm surprised to see you here Malcolm."

I rub the back of my neck with my left hand and feel my right hand involuntarily tighten around my briefcase.

"Why's that?" I ask.

He looks around with a sardonic expression.

"Well, Malcolm, because no one else is here. The place is a dangerous disaster zone, and also a crime scene. I'd be surprised to see anyone here."

"Ah, well yeah, I suppose," I concede. "I guess I just wanted to see it in the daylight. See how bad it really is."

"Oh," Upton says, sounding a little disappointed. "I guess I figured you were here to clean out your safe."

My heart stops.

"I'm sorry?"

"The safe in your apartment. I noticed you had a pretty substantial safe in your unit. I figured you must have some seriously important stuff in there. I know I'd want to get it out right away if it were me."

"Oh, that," I say, without breathing. "Nah, nothing in it."

Upton raises his eyebrows.

"Nothing in it? Nothing at all?"

"Nope, put it in there hoping there would be someday, but haven't gotten there yet."

Now he looks really confused.

"You build an expensive safe into the wall of an apartment you rent, just in case you ever had anything to put in it... someday?"

I feel myself getting squeamish. Time to get out of this conversation.

"I was supposed to come into some money this year, but it ended up not happening. What are you doing here Detective?"

He nods and smiles.

"Investigating, Mr. Karma. Always investigating."

"And have you found anything?" I ask.

He nods.

"I have," he says.

There's a long silence as we stare at each other.

"And..." I suggest.

"I'm not really at liberty to say yet," he says. "It was good to see you Malcolm. I'll be in touch if anything comes up."

He turns and walks across the parking lot just as my black Ford Flex pulls up. I climb in the back seat and breathe for the first time in ten minutes.

Chapter Seven

The sun is drowning in a bloody pool of sky when my car rolls into the motel parking lot. Elle is sitting in an aluminum lawn chair next to Robin and Erica. They're smiling and laughing in a pleasant and familiar way. Elle has some kind of red frozen drink in her hand that looks half melted in the summer heat.

I smile, glad that she's been able to take her mind off of things for a bit, able to find a moment of levity. My mind has been racing all day, juggling thoughts of Mica and Detective Upton and Alex Pilsen.

I can't quite make heads or tails of the way everyone is acting. If Mica wanted me dead, why the continued charade at the restaurant? Why tell me to leave town, to run essentially. Why not just have Don snap my neck at the bar and toss me out back with yesterday's fry oil? And was Upton suggesting, not so subtly, that he thought I had something to do with the fire? How could he have that already? What would lead him to that conclusion? The safe? I admit, I can see how a safe like mine in an apartment like that could look suspicious, but I hardly think it would be the most suspicious thing going on in the whole damn building.

Then there's Alex. The man was clearly surprised to see me, and unpleasantly surprised at that. But he still went out on a limb to help me out. He could have just as easily had me carried out in a dozen separate pieces, so why was he so ready to give me what I asked for? I'm generally not one to do a lot of extra, un-required thinking, but something in each of their encounters smells not unlike day old sushi.

I give the uber driver a cash tip and walk over to the trio of ladies lounging outside my room. Elle looks up at me with a wide warm smile and glassy eyes that tell me this isn't her first cocktail.

"How are you ladies tonight?" I ask, in an overly friendly tone.

"We are fine as Tahiti sand," Erica says.

"And your wife is sweet as my Grand Mama's peach cobbler," Robin adds.

Elle's focus seems to swim past me, then rocks back and her gaze meets my eyes.

"Mal, these girls are so much fun."

I smile.

"I may just leave you and run away with them," she teases.

"Is that so?" I say, glancing at Elle's new friends.

Robin gives me a devilish wink and Erica looks Elle up and down slowly, with a naughty smile.

"Well, I see how it is," I say.

"Sweet as peaches she may be, but I think my hands are full enough with this little lady. I can't imagine toting two of you broads around."

Elle puts on a wounded pout and stands herself up. She stumbles forward a few steps and falls into my arms.

"Well Mal," she says. "I guess my sweet peach is all yours."

She giggles in a way I haven't heard in years. There's a whisper in my ear before she straightens herself up and walks back to our room with a sway in her hips that has both of the ladies leaning over to watch.

"Thanks for keeping her company," I say. "It's been a rough day."

"It was our pleasure," says Robin.

"Go get some before you're stuck holding her hair," Erica adds.

I smile and turn towards our room. As I'm walking away Erica says, "Sleep safe Mal."

Elle rolls off of me, slick with sweat and various other natural fluids. She sprawls out across the cheap motel sheets and labors to catch her breath, giggling every so often as if what we've just done is funny in some way. Like we've gotten away with something. I stand up and walk to the bathroom to get a drink of water and throw her a towel.

She wipes her face, then stuffs the towel between her legs and rolls over on her stomach to face me. I bend over and take a long drink right from the faucet, then stand up and fill a glass. I turn and lean against the door frame staring at Elle, lit in a honey red glow from the end table lamp on her side of the bed. She grins at me with a satisfied expression.

"And what did you do today?" she says, playfully.

I laugh out loud and cross my arms.

"You mean, besides potentially impregnating my wife?"

"I know! Right?" she almost shouts.

I burst into laughter. Elle has always been able to make me laugh. It's funny to see a reserved, buttoned down professional get silly. It lightens the air and makes me relax a little.

"Shh," I caution her. "It's late and the walls here aren't exactly soundproof, or ya know, sound resistant."

She giggles and rolls over on her back, throwing her arms out wide and mocks shouting, "Hey Erica, Malcolm put a baby in me!"

"You're very funny," I say.

"I know, but seriously babe, we can't do that anymore. You need to wear something. We can't have a baby, we don't even have a place to live."

I roll my eyes.

"This is hardly permanent."

"Yeah, all the same, I was thinking it might not be a bad idea to give Mica a call and see if you can stay on a bit longer. Ya know, just until—"

"No." I shake my head.

"Mal, just—"

"Absolutely not," I almost shout. "Out of the question."

"Mal—"

"No!" I straighten up and take a step towards the bed. "It's not even an option, and besides, we don't need it. We're gonna be okay. Insurance is taking care of all the lost assets, car insurance is replacing car keys, and we'll have a new apartment in no time. I mean— hey, we could even buy a place. A house maybe."

She hops up on her knees and gives me a disapproving stare.

"I'm serious. We could move."

"Where?" she says.

"I don't know. How about Rockford," I offer. "Houses

are cheap there, and from what I hear they could really use a good prosecutor."

"Very funny," she says, cracking a smile.

"I have my moments. But in all seriousness Elle, a move could be a good thing. Maybe this fire, ya know, right after I quit my job, maybe it's a message telling us it's time to move on."

She looks at me questioningly for a long moment, then drops her shoulders with a sigh and smiles at me. She shakes her head wildly, letting her gorgeous brunette hair flail about like it's trying to leave the planet. She lets out a long guttural moan, then throws herself backwards onto the bed.

"Whatever! We can talk about it later. For now, come back here and do that thing to me again."

I stare at her madness and laugh.

"Which one?" I say.

"Duh," she say. "All of them."

Chapter Eight

W hen I wake up someone is knocking on the door to our room. I sit up slowly and chug the rest of the water in the glass next to the bed. The knocking continues, three taps at a time followed by a pause, presumably waiting for a reply. They are light friendly knocks, but they are persistent, and at this hour, unwelcome.

I wonder at the time and check my watch on the nightstand. Eight forty-five in the morning.

"Shit."

It's later than I thought. I glance around the room and see that Elle has already left.

I stand up and pull on some pants, commando style before answering the door, sans shirt. There are two gentlemen in front of me attempting to be well dressed. The first I already know, Detective Upton. The other man is taller, larger, and sporting a well kept, if slightly graying beard. Upton smiles at my expression.

"Mr. Karma," he says, formally.

"Detective," I say.

"This is Lt. Jeremy Rodden with the Fire Marshal's Office of Arson Investigation. He and I were hoping you had a moment to talk."

I glare skeptically at the two men, then open the door to its capacity and walk back to the bed to find a shirt.

I pull a white undershirt over my head and drop myself into the threadbare armchair in the corner of the room, positioning my arms to hide the wound from the other night.

"What's the word, gentlemen?"

Inspector Rodden looks around the room uncomfortably, like he's not sure where to sit or stand.

"We've determined the origin and cause for the fire at your apartment building," Detective Upton says.

"Well, that sounds like good news," I say.

Upton nods. Rodden wrinkles his brow and crosses his arms.

"Good news, sure. But the thing is Malcolm, the origin was in your unit and the mechanism seems to have been an explosive device."

I try to mimic genuine surprise.

"A device?" I say, affecting confusion. "What does that mean? Like a bomb?"

"Not like a bomb," Rodden chimes in, flatly. "A bomb. A gasoline bomb to be precise."

"What, like a Molotov cocktail?"

Upton smiles and shakes his head.

"No. No, not like that at all."

My confused expression changes from an act to the real thing.

"Well, what then?"

"It was rather large," Upton says, as if he's preparing me for unexpected bad news.

"At least twenty-five gallons," Rodden clarifies.

"And it was on a remote detonator," Upton says, suggestively.

I shift in my seat and immediately regret it.

"Do you gentlemen think maybe you could stop dancing around the issue and just come out with it? Are you telling me that someone was trying to kill us? That they were targeting us specifically?"

Rodden steps forward and uncrosses his arms.

"Mr. Karma, your apartment building was destroyed when a twenty-five gallon gasoline bomb was detonated inside your apartment unit. The bomb, which appears to have been located underneath your bed, was set off via a cellular device wired into the mechanism. The time of the detonation has been determined with a reliable level of specificity and accuracy due to numerous witnesses, both inside the building and outside."

Detective Upton takes a seat on the bed facing me. He leans in towards me and takes off his glasses.

Malcolm," he says in a low voice. "We ran your cell records and they show that you made a call to a pay-as-you-go burner phone at the exact moment of the explosion."

My jaw goes slack and small jewels of cold sweat dig their way out of my pores onto the surface of my forehead.

"We were on a walk," I say, sounding a little too defensive. "At the time of the fire, we were on a walk outside. I didn't even have my phone on me. It was in the apartment. It was destroyed in the fire."

"No Mr. Karma," Rodden says. "We have data showing that your phone was on and pinging off a cell tower less than half a mile from your apartment a full hour after the explosion."

My mouth goes dry and a chill runs through my body. I give a slow nod of my head and stare at the floor.

"I see."

"Is there anything you'd like to add or amend?" Upton asks.

"I kind of think I need to talk to my wife," I say.

Upton nods understandingly.

"Yeah, okay. Well, you'll get an opportunity to make that call," he says. "But if I were you I'd take that time to call a lawyer. Have them contact your wife for you."

"My wife is a lawyer," I bark at him.

"I know Malcolm, but as I'm sure she'll tell you, it's better not to represent yourself, even if you are a lawyer."

I look up into the detective's eyes.

"You're charging her too?"

"Her initial statement corroborated yours, so unless she's willing to recant that and give a different picture of events, we'll have to assume she's an accomplice."

I get up and Upton jumps to his feet. Rodden steps back into the open door frame.

"Easy fellas," I say.

"Mr. Karma, I'm going to have to ask you to turn around and place your hands on the back of your head."

I look dumbfounded at Upton. He has his right hand on his holstered weapon and the other up and half reaching towards me in a defensive posture. Rodden has his gun drawn, holding it with two hands, pointing at the floor in front of me. Slowly I raise my hands and put my palms on the back of my neck.

"Please turn around," Upton says, firmly.

I turn away from them and Upton ratchets one bracelet around my right wrist, then brings it down behind my back. He takes my left wrist and pulls it down to meet the right one and snaps the other cuff around it. He holds me by the chain between the cuffs and puts his other hand on my back between my shoulder blades and turns me towards the door.

"Malcolm Karma, you are under arrest for the crimes of arson and attempted murder. You have the right to remain silent..."

Surprisingly, I've never been to jail before. Unsurprisingly, it's not as glamorous as it is on TV. At least not at a suburban county jail. There are three guys in my lockup besides me and two of them are still drunk.

I called Elle with my phone call. I wanted to make sure she was able to get out of the office before the cops showed up. I don't imagine it would do her career a whole lot of good to be dragged out of the State's Attorney's office in handcuffs. Thankfully I got to her in time.

Apparently she was able to get out of the office, call a lawyer for me and negotiate her own surrender before anyone showed up at work. I got all this from Ms. Allie Stanley Esq, the lawyer Elle set me up with. I haven't heard from Elle since then.

Allie spent a quick fifteen minutes with me, on the phone, getting the gist of what went down then told me she'd be over to see me as soon as she had a chance. She sounded young, which isn't necessarily a bad thing. The problem is, she's not my lawyer. She's *our* lawyer, which means I'm limited in what I can share with her. I can't, for example, tell her that it was Mica who had my apartment blown up. That she was trying to kill me because I left her mob of secret illegal enforcers. In short, I can't tell her the truth.

I did tell her that bail was my priority. Since I can't tell her what's going on I need to get out and figure it out for myself.

"Malcolm Karma!"

The cold metallic voice of the guard echoed in the concrete chamber, making my eardrums ring.

I stand up and raise my hand like I'm in the third grade.

"Yeah, that's me, officer."

"Pack your crap man, you're outta here."

"I'm what?" I ask, confused and a little nervous.

"Outta here. Now!"

"Where am I going?"

"As if I give a fuck," he barks, dismissively.

I barely have time to process before they hand me an envelope full of everything I had in my pockets this morning and boot me out into the empty parking lot.

I walk out into the sun and look back at the building.

"What the fuck is going on?" I wonder out loud.

"I told you to fucking leave."

I spin around like a top. Behind me Mica is standing about a dozen feet away in a sharp, navy blue skirt suit and red heels. The world wobbles around me, almost bringing me to my knees. After I catch my balance I immediately scan the area for one or more of her goons.

I'm stunned, partly because I've never seen Mica outside the city before. Hell, I've never seen her outside the restaurant before. But, also, and mostly, because I've never seen her dressed like this before. Mica is a barefoot and bell-bottoms kind of woman. Seeing her dressed like she's running a corporate takeover is unsettling in a very non-specific way.

"What the hell are you doing here?" I say.

"I told you to leave town. I thought I was pretty clear. It cost me a lot of chits to get you out of that building, and this isn't even the city. You stick around any longer and I won't have the pull to get you out even if I was so inclined."

"I don't understand," I say.

Mica crosses the space between us and hands me a large brown envelope from inside her purse.

"I had Don get it out of your motel room before the cops had a chance to find it."

I squeeze the package and feel the unmistakeable shape of a handgun.

"I'm assuming that was for me," she says. "That was misguided of you, but more than likely you'll still need it, so I suggest you keep it on you."

I squint and my mind does somersaults trying to connect the dots.

"Mal, it's not important that you understand everything. What is important is that you don't end up in jail. That's important, so go get your wife and take a little trip. Mexico is supposed to be great this time of year."

I just stare at her blankly.

"Nod your head if you understand."

I nod.

Mica turns and starts to walk away, then pauses.

"Mal,"

"Yeah?"

"Those ladies. The ones at the motel."

"Erica and Robin?" I say.

"They aren't your friends Mal. Don't let them know where you're going."

I frown.

"Now get gone. Stay gone."

Chapter Nine

I'm staring out the window of a Cadillac. We're parked under a huge oak tree on a residential street, across from a small brick house. It's the address that came up when I googled Allie Stanley Law Offices. At first I assume my phone made a mistake and gave me her home address, then I notice a small white sign posted on the brick wall next to the mailbox.

I scratch my head while I lean forward and squint at the sign. It seems unlikely that this is who Elle would choose to represent us.

"I beat her a lot."

I jump backwards and my heart tries to climb out of my

throat as a young blond woman sticks her head in the window of the car.

"Hi!" She says, cheerfully.

I choke and cough, trying to catch my breath.

"You were trying to figure out why Elle had you come here, right?"

I glare back and bob my head.

"Yeah, I suppose."

"Right, guess I can't blame you, although, you'd be surprised how similar pet rescue and defense law can be."

"I'm sure I would," I stammer.

"Right, and well, I just like making jewelry, so I decided to put it on the sign, but to be honest I'm not really all that good at it."

"How did—"

"You've been parked out here staring at my house for like fifteen minutes," she says. "Did you think I wasn't going to notice a big black Cadillac?"

"I guess I didn't think about it," I confess.

"Right, seems like there's been quite a bit of that going around, huh?"

"I'm sorry?"

"I beat her a lot," Allie says and opens up the car door and climbs in the back next to me. "That's why Elle hired me. She's a pretty good lawyer, that wife of yours, but I beat her all the damn time."

"Okay," I say.

She smiles at me.

"Right, so, you're in a lot of trouble Mal."

I nod.

"I gather that much, but why?"

"Mmm, right," she sighs. "I suppose we'll get to that too,

in a minute, but right now you're in trouble because I can't be your lawyer."

"What?"

"Yeah," she sounds disappointed. "But you really need me Mal. Like for real, I don't think anyone else can help you."

"Okay," I say. "So, then, why can't you be my lawyer?"

"Because," she says, like it's the most obvious thing in the world. She leans in close to me and whispers, "Your wife."

"Oh," I say, the fog only partly lifting. "Oh, you can't represent both of us?"

"Well, yeah," she snorts. "I mean, you know, legally I can, but..." she trails off and makes wide eyes at me. I look back completely lost.

She gives me a small pout and sighs again.

"Excuse me sir?" she says, leaning forward into the front seat of the car. "Excuse me, would you mind leaving the car for a bit? Ya know, just take a little walk?"

The Uber driver looks back at her like she's on crack.

"Uh, no. This is my car lady, and y'all have been sitting in here too long anyway. Why don't you get out and take a walk?"

Allie frowns and scoots closer to him.

"Actually," she says. "Since I'm an officer of the court, and this man here is my client, under US Statute 473.21B any space that we occupy together becomes a protected council space and we can demand privacy at any time, even if the space is owned privately by a third party. Moreover, failure on your part to comply with a request for privacy entitles me to file a Higgins motion in federal court asking that you be—"

"Okay! Okay, fuck. I get it. I'm leaving. How long do you need?"

"Fifteen minutes would be great. Thank you so much."

The driver shuts off the engine and gets out of the car, grumbling something about none of this being worth it.

"Wow, I have to say, I didn't know any of that either."

"Any of what?" she asks, in an airy tone.

"That stuff you just said. About protected spaces and section B12 or whatever."

She laughs.

"Oh, that. That's all bullshit. I just made it up. I just wanted him to leave so we could talk privately."

I look back at her in awe.

"Look Mal," Allie says. "I need to help you, but I'm hampered by Elle not knowing that you're involved."

"I'm sorry, what?" I blurt.

"Mal, she assumes that this is about her. About one of her cases, but you and I know that this is about you and your relationship with Mica Kole."

I feel like someone just hit me in the gut with a baseball bat.

"Uh, Mica was my— I mean, I used to work for her. Uh, at the restaurant."

"Mal, this is what I'm talking about."

I run my fingers through my hair and take a deep breath.

"Mal, twenty-five gallons of gasoline was placed under your bed, and then detonated by a phone call made from your cell."

I look at Allie, who is now staring at me with dead eyes.

"Mal, I can help you. I can, but first you have to tell Elle what you do and who you do it for."

"I can't do that."

Allie puts a hand on my shoulder.

"I know Mal, but you're gonna have to."

There's a long silence.

"Come on kiddo," she says. "We'll do it together."

She opens the car door and we climb out onto the serene suburban street, under the warm midday sun.

"Ooh, I know what. You can buy her some jewelry, women love jewelry. I'll show you what I've got and help you pick something out. She's a December stone, right?"

I follow her up her driveway towards the front door.

"Oh hey, by the way Mal, how'd you get out of jail so fast?

"Ha," I laugh out loud. "Actually, Mica got me out."

Allie stops walking.

"Oh Mal, you are in a lot of trouble."

———

Elle stares at me with cow's eyes as I go through the story. I explain everything. How I met Mica, the kinds of things I did for her, the other people under her thumb, and how I got out. I tell her about the money I got when she let me go, and that she told me to get out of town. I tell her about the gun from Alex Pilsen and about Don Lorah retrieving it from the hotel room. I explain the situation with the safe and Detective Upton and the Fire Marshal Inspector. I finish with who got me out of jail and what she said when she did.

It's pretty quiet after I finish. Elle looks away from me and avoids looking back. She's got a peculiar frown on her face that I've seen many times before. I call it her thinking face and it's never good news if it's there because of you. I assume she's angry, but that's an emotion not betrayed by her expression.

After a while Elle lets out a long sigh, runs her fingers through her hair and stands up. She paces back and forth in Allie's office, pausing to say something, then not finding the words, goes back to pacing without saying anything at all. This cycle repeats for what seems like hours.

"Malcolm," Allie finally says.

"Are you sure that's really his name?" Elle spits, under her breath.

"Elle—"

"Mal," Allie interrupts. "I think, well, you, you think, uh, maybe I need to talk to Elle alone for a minute."

I glance at her, then look back at Elle who is still facing away from me. I stand up silently and walk out of the room.

I pace around the small reception space for a bit, then wander out and find the living room of the house. It's meticulously clean and tastefully decorated in a modern country motif. I wander through the dining room and kitchen until I find a large screened in porch out back.

Two of the walls are lined with a dozen or so clean, stainless steel cages, each containing a small to medium sized dog, yapping or barking respectively. The last cage on the end has a slightly larger dog with seven itty bitty puppies suckling at its tits.

The mother dog appears to be some kind of Yellow Lab mutt, as do six of the puppies, but the seventh pup looks a little lost. It's shaped the same as the others, but with the coloring and markings of a German Shepherd.

I open the cage and pick him up off his mother. He wiggles in my hands and gives a chirpy bark. I nuzzle him to my face and kiss the soft hair on the top of his head.

"Ooh, ooh, ooh!" Comes the flighty excited voice of my lawyer. "Ya know what women love more than jewelry?"

I look up and see Elle standing next to her staring down at me.

"Puppies!" Allie squeals.

I smile.

"What about it Mal?" Elle says softly, her voice cracking slightly. "Ya wanna get a dog?"

I look at her with all my love and nod once.

"What's this fella's name?" I ask.

"Actually,"Allie says. "I've been calling him Malcolm."

"What do you know about Gavin Gayle?" Allie asks.

I feel my muscles stiffen and my stomach somersault. Elle just laughs.

"Come on Allie," she says. "I see where you're going with this, but Gavin Gayle is a story, like Resurrection Mary, or the Hull House devil baby. It's a morality tale about where things can go when government corruption gets out of control.

"Besides, the parallels aren't quite there. Mica is a restauranteur that, apparently, runs a gang of thugs on the side. She's not some big city State's Attorney using her power to create a personal assassin, and Mal's never been to prison."

I shift in my seat. I, too, see where Allie is going, but I immediately know she's right and Elle is looking at it the wrong way.

"My thing is," I chime in. "I'm starting to get the feeling that it isn't Mica who tried to kill us. Tried to kill me. I'm actually starting to suspect that she really is trying to help."

Allie nods.

"I agree," she says. "But that doesn't mean she's not involved, or that she's safe. If anything, it suggests that she does know what's going on and probably, exactly who's behind it."

"But it's just a *story*!" Elle insists, again. "None of this is real. We are in real trouble. Real danger. We need to be looking at real solutions."

Allie gives a pitying smile to Elle and sighs.

"Elle, you'd be surprised how many of the urban legends and old wives tales you hear are actually based in reality. Gavin was, well, he is a real man and the stories you've heard are more truth than fiction."

"I highly doubt—fc"

"Elle, you're just going to have to take my word on this one. Gavin is in the past, he's not active anymore, but I promise you friend, he exists and he did exactly what you've heard he did."

"How do you know?" Elle asks.

"Do you really imagine that's something I'd be able to tell you Elle?"

Elle frowns.

"If I told you the tooth fairy was real, but that you'd just have to take my word for it, would you?"

"Well, if you'd just introduced me to the Easter Bunny," Allie looks at me, then back to Elle. "Then yeah, I probably would."

Elle stays quiet.

"Look," Allie says. "What you have to understand is that Gavin was a symptom, not of a corrupt individual, but of an entrenched culture of corruption. That's not something that goes away overnight."

Elle nods.

"When Gavin got out, it left a hole. An empty role that the culture didn't know how to fill any other way."

"Okay," Elle says. "But we already know from Mal that Mica has a whole team of guys like him out there doing this shit. Him getting out isn't leaving that same kind of hole in the system."

Allie shakes her head in frustration.

"You're not getting it Elle."

"What am I not getting?"

I stand up and walk over to Elle and put my hand on her shoulder.

"Elle, sweetheart,"

She looks up at me with frightened and confused eyes.

"Elle, I'm not the one that replaced Gavin in the system. I'm not the one that filled that hole. Mica is."

Part Two

Mica

Chapter Ten

Mica stood in the long florescent hallway feeling the tingle of anticipation run over her skin like a thousand tiny ants. The chaos and activity were unmistakeable, it was the first day of school, but more importantly, it was her first day of senior year.

She took her time walking to her locker, allowing herself the opportunity to take it all in. Letting her brain make the memories that she would, no doubt, carry with her into adulthood. The way she saw it, there were turning points in a person's life. Periods of time that pointed you in the direction you would travel down for years afterwards. Senior year of high school was one of those times.

She'd worked hard to set herself up for an amazing year. She got herself elected treasurer of the student body. A position that, in her mind, was more prestigious than Student Body President. It had all the hallmarks of the executive branch, but it also had the inherent responsibility of raising and managing the cashflow of a large organization. A big plus on her application to the Department of Economics at the University of Chicago.

She was also about to test for her black belt in Taek-wondo, an achievement she'd been working on for eight years. She was especially proud of this because she'd studied at one of the most difficult dojos in the city. It was common these days for dojos to pass students up the levels as long as they showed even the most rudimentary ability to mimic the forms and, of course, had the ability to pay the testing fee. But her master wouldn't pass his students up until they demonstrated an absolute mastery of, not only the forms, but the discipline and mindset associated with the rank. Meditation was key, as was knowledge of the history of the art and a respect for your peers. As a result, she often bested even those ranked well above her in competitions.

The final piece to her trifecta for the perfect senior year was the perfect boyfriend. Mark Farley asked her out halfway through the summer. It wasn't exactly unexpected. She had spent a month and a half flirting and dropping not so subtle hints that she was interested.

He was handsome. Not an athlete, but in good shape and very smart. He headed the debate team, was editor of the school newspaper and yearbook, and was ranked third on the school's chess team. On top of all that, he was English. Right off the boat English too, having just moved to The States two and a half years ago, in the middle of their freshman year. She loved to listen to him talk, his accent was divine.

She spun the dial on her locker, grinning like an idiot with eager anticipation of the year to come. A pair of hands slipped over her eyes and a voice in an awful, fake American accent said, "Guess who Mica!"

She laughed.

"Well, this must be my strong American boyfriend Joey!"

The hands fell to her waist and spun her around.

"That's not funny young lady," Mark said, shaking a finger at her.

"You're literally one month older than me, old man," Mica said, rolling her eyes.

"Hey, a lot can happen in a month."

"I kind of doubt that a single month could be that life altering."

"Well, give me a dark room and a soft bed and I can make five minutes change your life."

Mica leaned back against her locker and crossed her arms.

"It's funny that you think that makes you sound good," she said.

"What?" Mark said, not following.

"Oh, did I say funny? Sorry, I meant sad."

"Oh come on Mica, you know what I meant."

Mica pouted her lip.

"Yes, sadly I do," she said, leaned forward and kissed him on the cheek.

"Mica!" Another voice shouted, from down the hall.

A petite blonde girl in a cheer uniform top, and black sweatpants was running down the hall waving a pink slip of paper at them.

"Hey Whitney," Mica said with a giggle. "Take a breath girl, it's like seven in the morning. Nobody's ready for your energy this early."

"Sorry," Whitney said holding out the piece of paper. "But the fundraiser flyers are done. They need to be picked up from the printer today after school. Can you drive?"

Whitney Hemsath was the Secretary of the student body and captain of the cheer squad, all of which despite the fact that she didn't have a car.

"Damn, I can't," Mica spat. "My parents have my car today. They're uh, getting the grease replaced or some shit."

Whitney sighed.

"I can drive," Mark offered.

Mica and Whitney both turned and stared at Mark with their mouths hanging open.

"You know the steering wheel is on the left side of the car, right?" Mica said, dryly.

"This coming from the girl that doesn't know that cars need oil!" Mark jabbed.

"The printer is on the south side of the city," Whitney added. "You okay with that?"

"Jesus girls," Mark said. "We're getting paper from the press, what's gonna happen?"

———————

School let out at 2:40, and by five minutes to three Mica, Whitney, and Mark were squished into Mark's twenty year old red Ford Escort. They headed down the fifteen mile long, County Highway that connected the North and South Sides of the city. The car was small and smelled of potent teenage boy and cheap pink mall perfume. The radio played loudly, spilling pop punk ballads out the open windows that served as the only air conditioning in the vehicle.

Mark drove the car wearing a shit eating grin. Mica and Whitney shouted day one gossip at each other over the squeal of guitars and the roar of the wind pouring in the open windows.

The weather was still warm and the afternoon sun made their skin and hair glow. The mood was light and jovial, full of summertime freedom and new school year hopefulness. Then they pulled off the smooth winding ribbon of asphalt that wrapped around the Great Lake and found themselves in a place they didn't recognize.

The South Side was a gray place. No effort was made by the municipal government to maintain greenery. Places that should be all trees, grass, and cedar chips were, instead, poured concrete and wrought iron fences. The sky seemed to go steely and the atmosphere transformed to one of frigidity, even in the late summer swelter.

The trio of teenagers went abruptly quiet, turning the radio off and rolling up the windows despite the sticky wet air. They leaned forward in their seats, eyeing every street sign, anxious to find a place of purpose. Desperate to remove themselves from the category of people who didn't belong.

After ten minutes and two wrong turns they found their way to the print shop and pulled up to the wide black gate and the stainless steel intercom box.

"What's it to ya?" came the twangy voice on the other end of the wire.

Whitney leaned over Mark's shoulder from the back seat and shouted.

"Hi there. Yeah, we're here from Henry Higgins High to pi-"

A loud buzzer sounded and the gate shook and slowly slid open.

"Rude!" Whitney said.

"Just keep it simple, okay?" Mark said.

"I thought you weren't scared," Mica teased.

"I just want to be professional," Mark said.

Mica chortled.

"You're seventeen," Whitney jabbed. "The only plastic

in your wallet is your library card. I think you're a couple yards short of professional."

"Huh?" Mark grunted.

"It's a football metaphor sweetheart," Mica said.

The gate clanged at the end of its rail and Mark pulled in and found a parking spot. The kids hopped out and went into the stout brick building single file and silent.

At the desk was a round woman with rust colored hair and enough freckles to make the prospect of melanoma cross your mind. She looked up at the teens with annoyance, then leaned under her desk.

"Hi, we're here to pick up-"

The woman dropped a box the size of a sheet of copier paper and roughly five inches thick on the desk in front of her, then went back to typing on her computer. Mica picked up the box, said thank you, and turned to walk out the door. Mark turned to follow, but Whitney didn't move.

"You're very rude," she said to the receptionist.

The woman behind the counter paused, looked at Whitney, then raised her eyebrows in a manner that clearly said, "what's your point?"

"We could take our business elsewhere."

The round woman crossed her arms and sat back in her chair.

"Listen Barbie, our minimum order here is ten thousand prints. That's twenty of those boxes your friend is holding. We only do this shitty order for your school because the owner's daughter went there like a hundred years ago or something. And even at that he gives you a ridiculous discount. So sweetie, if you want to go to Kinko's be my guest."

Whitney stared at the woman with horror painted across her face.

"Ta ta," the lady said, and went back to her computer.

Whitney took a deep breath, pulled back her shoulders, and walked out the front door. Mark chuckled and Mica punched him in the shoulder.

"Ow," Mark said.

"Don't be a girl," Mica mocked, and they walked out.

Back at the car Whitney slumped in the back seat.

"We are never going back there."

"Well, it doesn't sound like that's any skin off their neck."

Mark started the car and the big black gate slid open. The trio sat silently as the small car rolled out of the lot and onto the broken, uneven pavement of the street. The gate closed slowly behind them. They made it a block before the engine cut out and the car stopped.

"Mark."

"Whitney, please don't start. Please, just don't-"

"Mark, why is the car stopped."

"We're out of gas," Mica said in her calm angry voice.

"Mark?"

"Whitney, just-"

"Mark are we out of gas? Mica? Are you serious? Mark?"

"For fuck's sake Whitney! Yes! We're out of gas! I thought I could make it back to the highway, but I guess I was off a bit."

"Jesus fuck Mark!" Whitney screamed. "What were you going to do then?"

"There's a station there. I was going to fill up then."

"Jesus Christ! What the fuck! Didn't your parents teach you not to run your tank down so low?"

"Says the girl without a car," Mark shouted back.

"Yeah, and even I fucking know that, ass hole. Shit, Mica, why are you so calm?"

"It's happened before."

The car went silent.

"It's what?" Whitney said softly.

"Thanks for that hun," Mark said.

Mica looked at him with dagger eyes.

"Really? I wouldn't start shifting aggravations right now darling."

"Mark, I'm not in a happy place right now. Mica, why do you date this loser anyway?"

"That's a question worth visiting once we're back on the road," Mica said. "Right now it's more important to find some gas."

"Maybe we should go back to the print shop," Mark offered.

Whitney swung a wide arc and slapped Mark hard behind the ear.

"I think that's a no babe," Mica said.

"I guess I'll walk up the road to the station then," Mark said.

"Have fun with that," Whitney sneered.

"No way," Mica injected. "You're not walking around this neighborhood alone."

"Don't you have tripple-A?"

"I don't have a CD player Princess Moneybags."

"Then y'all better start walkin'."

Mica smiled at Whitney.

"You're not staying here alone either."

"What?" Whitney shouted.

"We're all walking," Mica said.

"The fuck I am."

"Curse all you want, you're not staying here alone. We stick together, and that means we're all going to get gas."

"But what about my car?" Mark protested.

"It's out of gas darling."

"But my rims..."

"Jesus Mark, you drive a twenty year old Escort. No one wants your fucking hubcaps," Whitney said.

There was a long moment of silence, then the three of them, moving as one, climbed out of the car and began walking quietly up the street towards the highway.

The station ended up being a full mile and a half away. They were sticky and exhausted by the time they walked into the store. Mark had eight dollars on him which, after buying the gas can, only left a buck fifty for actual gasoline. Mica paid another five fifty which filled up the can and got them each a bottle of water.

"You're a class act Mark," Whitney whispered under her breath as Mica slid the cash under the three inch thick bulletproof glass to the attendant.

They walked back towards the car with silent animosity hanging over them, sipping their water and staring at the ground. Five minutes later they couldn't even see the station and the sun was starting to hug the tops of the buildings to their right.

Another three minutes found them in the middle of a five way intersection inhabited by a group of twenty-somethings. Four of them trying their best to ignore a fifth that was clearly high on something other than life. He was putting on a show, desperate for attention and acting like he wanted the world to think less of him. He was making pistols with his fingers and holding them sideway like he'd seen in the movies.

The other four seemed unimpressed and were waving him off and mocking him. Mica and her group saw the commotion and began making a wide arc around the intersection. The star of the show noticed though, and shouted.

"Awe, hey girlies, lookin' fine. Why don't you come over here and party with us?"

One of the quiet kids smacked him on the back of the head.

"You stupid pedo mother-fucker, those are just kids."

"They look old enough for me," the piece of shit said, and made grotesque gestures at the girls with his hips.

The four younger boys all made various faces of disgust and left the intersection down a residential street. The remaining kid flipped them all the bird and started walking towards Mica and Whitney.

"Hey sugar, looks like there's more for me."

The three stranded teenagers avoided looking up at the thug and kept walking, but the asshole jogged up and stood in their path.

"How 'bout it ladies? You wanna party?"

"Mark, you gonna do something?" Whitney whispered.

Mark put down the gas can and his bottle of water and stepped forward putting out his hand.

"Why don't you just leave us alone?"

"Us?" the thug said. "I ain't talkin' to your ass in any case white boy."

Mark squinted, confused.

"You're white too..."

"Uh, you're white too," the guy said in a mockingly nasal voice.

"Just leave us-"

"Shut the fuck up!" The delinquent shouted in Mark's face.

Mark reached a hand out and laid it on the boy's shoulder. The kid went wide eyed and crazy. He blew a lungful of air out of pursed lips and cold cocked Mark square in the nose. Blood sprayed across Mark's face and the boy's fist. He let out a deep guttural moan and collapsed on the ground. He screamed and sobbed holding his broken face. Whitney shrieked and turned to run, but the boy caught her by her uniform collar and threw her hard to the ground. Her head bounced hard off the rough concrete and a deep scarlet pool of blood began to form under her golden blonde hair.

Mica took a step backwards, fighting the urge to dart away and trying to keep her breath even like she'd been taught in her martial arts classes. The boy stepped forward twice as fast and reached an eager hand out for her hair. Mica grabbed his wrist with two hands, turned it, ducked under the arm and yanked it up behind his back. She heard a loud crack in his shoulder and a pop in his elbow, then he screamed. She kept pulling until he dropped to his knees, then stepped back and kicked her heel hard into the back of his head. His body fell forward and she heard his nose crack against the pavement. Then she dropped down, letting gravity take her full weight, and landed her elbow straight on his limp spine. She heard the sound of a thick tree branch breaking and the boy emptied his lungs all at once.

Mica laid there hyperventilating against the boy's unmoving body. Soon there were police, then ambulances, then darkness and sleep. In the morning there was her.

Chapter Eleven

The Sunlight snuck in, in skinny slices through sterile, white vertical blinds. It made jaunty patterns across the blank, white wall at the foot of Mica's bed.

She found it odd to be waking up on her back. It was an unnatural position for her, and uncomfortable. She always slept on her side and woke up with her left hand numb, tucked under the pillow in just the wrong way. Now, on her back, her left hand was stretched out and away from her, but still with that familiar numbness.

She gave her arm a shake to try and get the blood moving, but found that she couldn't move it more than an inch or two in any direction. It was stuck in place and there was something wrapped around it cutting off the circulation to her hand.

Groggily, she tugged at her arm again, then opened her eyes to see what exactly she was stuck on. She had a headache and her body was sore. For a moment she wondered what had happened to make her ache all over. Had she been in a car accident?

Then it happened. The rush of memory like waves crashing on the jagged rocks of reality. She bolted upright, her hand stubbornly staying where it was and pulling painfully at the muscles and tendons in her elbow and shoulder.

She screamed.

She was in a tiny, sparse hospital room. There was a whiteboard at the foot of her bed with two names scribbled in fading red marker. The bed was long and narrow with sturdy rails on either side. A small remote near her right hand had a single red button labeled call. Her left hand was attached to the rail by heavy steel handcuffs.

She scanned the room frantically, trying to figure out where she was and how she arrived there. She began pressing the call button over and over again. A moment later two nurses burst into the room. They were putting their hands on her. One was shouting numbers and meaningless words at the other. They were reading screens and scratching messy letters on lined paper stuck to metal clipboards.

A policeman stepped into the room, his right hand resting uneasily on his pistol. He asked in an urgent tone if everything was alright. When no answer came back he seemed to evaluate the situation for himself and stepped back outside the room.

The older nurse put down her clipboard and took a seat on the edge of Mica's bed. She grabbed her hands and pushed them gently into her lap and held them firmly. She began speaking very softly in a firm, but caring voice while she stroked the backs of Mica's hands.

"Mica."

Mica's eyes were wide and wild. She swung her head around in frantic, jerky motions.

"Where am I? What happened? There was a man. He tried to- where's Whitney? Where am I?"

The nurse put a soft hand on the side of Mica's face and brought her eyes in line with her own.

"Mica, you're in Jackson Park Hospital. You were in an altercation. You're going to be alright, but I need you to calm down now."

Mica took a couple heaping gulps of air and stopped screaming. She stared at the woman next to her and waited, waited for someone to tell her what was going on. The officer who had been in the room earlier stepped back in now that the screaming had stopped.

"We all good in here?"

The nurse nodded without breaking eye contact with Mica. The officer nodded and stepped back out into the hall. Mica heard the crackle of his radio and his voice saying "three-seven-one at J-P-H reporting. The girl is awake. Repeat, Mica Kole is awake."

"It's okay sweetheart. You're alright. Just a minor concussion. You're going to be okay."

Mica breathed deeply. She wasn't a doctor, but she had friends who had had concussions before, and no one ever said it wasn't a big deal.

"Where are my friends?" she asked. "Where are Whitney and Mark? Why am I handcuffed to the bed? Where are my parents? What's going on?"

"Right now just rest," the nurse said, in a sweet but forceful tone. "I'll get someone who knows the answers to your questions soon, but please try and rest."

Mica frowned.

"Where are my parents? Why aren't they here?"

The nurse patted Mica's hand.

"Your parents are here. You'll be able to see them soon, I promise. Just get some rest. You really need to rest."

The nurse put a hand on Mica's shoulder and stood up.

"I'll get you some food."

"But-"

The woman walked out of the room and closed the door behind her.

The food came about twenty minutes later, but with no answers. No one could, or would, say what had happened to her or her friends, why she was handcuffed, or why she couldn't talk to her parents. That was the strangest part. Her parents were, what was commonly called, helicopter parents. If she was fifteen minutes late getting home from school they would be calling everyone in the directory trying to find her.

There was just no way that she could be so seriously hurt without her parents beating her to the hospital and standing watch over her until she was released. Also, she was under eighteen, so Mica was pretty sure it was illegal for the hospital to refuse her requests to speak with her parents. Yet that's exactly what they had done over and over again since she had arrived.

After she finished eating she pressed the call button to have the nurse come and retrieve the tray. This time when she came in Mica would not let her leave without letting her talk with her parents, but the nurse didn't come. Instead, the police officer opened the door and stepped into the room. He gave a quick look around and nodded to himself, then approached the bed. There was a quick inspection of the handcuffs securing her to the rail, then he took the tray and headed for the door.

"Hey, thanks for the help. I was worried they were getting loose," Mica shouted at him.

The cop didn't react, he just carried the tray and disappeared out the door.

"Everyone here is so helpful," she said under her breath.

Before the door to her room shut, it was stopped and swung back open in a long slow arc. As it opened a new woman walked into the room. Mica hadn't seen her before, but she knew for sure she wasn't a doctor or a nurse. In fact, she was certain that this woman didn't work for the hospital at all. This woman didn't look like someone who helped people, she looked like someone who owned them.

Tall, but not overly so, just above average if she had to guess. But that was the only thing average about her. She was beautiful, but with an icy quality that was intimidating and borderline frightening. She had long legs that jutted out from a form fitting skirt ending just above her knees. Her blouse was black silk and sleeveless with a neckline that was professional, but only just. Her skin was tan and smooth and taut against her collarbone. She had a slender neck interrupted by a black choker that somehow defied the odds and made her look sophisticated. Her high cheekbones were dusted conservatively with rouge and black horn rimmed glasses that drew attention to her deep brown eyes.

Mica shuddered. In her life she had never seen a woman, a person, who walked so casually but carried such authority. She had no idea who this woman was, but she knew one thing, She was afraid of her.

"Mica, I'm State's Attorney Autumn Faraday," the woman said, in a voice soft and cold.

Mica tried to speak, but she found herself choking on her words, unable to articulate anything useful.

"Don't worry young lady, you'll have plenty of time to talk. For now, why don't you just listen."

Mica stared back, unmoving, unresponsive.

"Good, as I said, I'm S.A. Faraday. I know you've been asking a lot of questions, and I'll do my best to answer them as soon as I get some answers of my own. Does that make sense."

Mica's mouth was dry and she was feeling light headed. Her heart started to racing and she was beginning to sweat.

"My-" she coughed. "My parents. Can I see my parents first?"

The woman smiled.

"I can't legally stop you from seeing your parents seeing as how you're under eighteen. God knows they are eager to see you. But why don't you listen to what I have to say and then decide if you want to see them first or not."

Mica frowned. Nothing would make her want to wait to see her parents. She took a deep breath, but the woman cut her off.

"Trust me Mica, there's two ways this moment can go and you're going to prefer to hear what they are before you go making choices you can't take back."

"What's going on?" Mica choked.

The woman pulled up a chair and sat down. She crossed her legs and her arms and leaned back in the seat.

"Mica, you're in the hospital because you suffered a head injury during an altercation yesterday afternoon. You're handcuffed because during this altercation you assaulted and killed an undercover police officer."

Mica's heart stopped. She felt her face drain of its blood and her whole body went cold. The woman sitting across from her seemed to disappear down a long tunnel. Her face was blurry and indistinguishable from the souroundings. Her voice was thin and hollow as if it were very far away.

"My friends," Mica started, but couldn't put the rest of it together.

"You're friends," the woman said coldly. "Whitney Hemsath died this morning due to complications surrounding the head injury she sustained. Mark Farley is stable, but in a medically induced coma while he is recovering from his injuries."

Mica felt like she was going to throw up. She didn't remember Mark getting hurt that bad. A bump on the head, probably a concussion like she had, but she couldn't see how that would wind him up in a coma.

"Mica, here's your choice. This is the moment that will decide the rest of your life. I need you to listen very carefully, and think very clearly. Do you think you can do that?"

Mica couldn't move, she couldn't think at all, let alone clearly. What was happening? How was this the moment that would decide her whole life?

"Mica, I need you to nod your head if you understand me."

Mica nodded.

"Good. Listen closely. I can go out into the waiting room right now and get your parents. I can bring them in here. Then, with them as witnesses I can call in the officer from earlier. I'll give you a moment with them, and then, in front of your mother and father I will place you under arrest for the attempted purchase of heroin, and the murder of an undercover police officer."

Mica's eyes went wild. She opened her mouth to scream at this woman, to tell her that she never tried to buy any drugs. That she was trying to avoid the whole situation. She was protecting herself and her friends, but the woman uncrossed her arms and held up her hand.

"That's what I'll do. You can say what you like, but you have nothing to contradict me and I have a lot of evidence, including statements from the other young men who were there at the time of the altercation."

Mica's mouth shut and she felt the room start to spin.

"So that's Option A," the woman said. "Now, Option B is I call that nice officer in here now, before I get your parents, and he uncuffs you. We get you set up nice and straight, clean you up a bit, call your parents in here and send you home to enjoy your senior year of high school."

Mica looked bewildered.

"I don't understand," she said.

Autumn crossed her arms again.

"It's simple Mica. Either you choose now to spend the rest of your life in prison for murder, or you choose to go home with mommy and daddy. Is that too much to wrap your brain around?"

"But-" Mica's voice was soft and horse.

"Oh right, the but," the woman said. "The but is that if you choose to go home, choose to leave this dreadful mistake you made in the past, if you choose that path, the luggage you carry is that you will work for me. I lost a good officer at your hands Mica. It's up to you to replace him."

Mica bit her lower lip.

"You want me to become a police officer?"

The woman laughed.

"No Mica. Not a police officer. I need you for something special, but here's the thing Mica, you need to do everything I ask. No questions. Also, you can never tell anyone, anyone, that you work for me or what you do. If you do, if you tell anyone at all, even a single soul, I'll put you in prison for life. I'll seek the death penalty. I will leave your parents childless and alone wondering where they went wrong."

Mica couldn't breathe.

"So, what is it kid? Shall I call in your parents and read you your rights, or shall we get that officer in here to uncuff you?"

Mica stared at Autumn with fear and disbelief.

"Mica?"

She nodded.

"Good choice girl. Good choice."

Chapter Twelve

Mica stepped through the enormous Gothic arch at the entrance of her high school. The sun was high in the clear blue sky. The magnolia tree in the middle of the circle driveway was starting to show tiny pink buds. It was the start of spring break and Mica was looking forward to a week of rest and rejuvenation.

Senior year had been daunting thus far. Even more than she had expected. A respite from term papers, college applications, and the relentless expectations for her to pin down a life plan was just what she needed.

The beginning of the year had been so devastating. She still felt the loss of her friend Whitney and her boyfriend who still hadn't recovered. Added to that was the looming threat of *The Woman*. That's how Mica thought of her, Autumn Faraday was simply *The Woman*.

For weeks Mica had waited, living on pins and needles. Wondering when *The Woman* would show up, wanting her for whatever it was she had planned. She lay awake at night trying to imagine what kind of work it was *The Woman* had planned for her. Clearly it wasn't anything good. In fact, she assumed it was something decidedly bad. Why else would she have insisted on such secrecy. Why else would the penalty for betrayal be so severe? The question that haunted Mica was a matter of degree. Bad to what extent would the request be?

Obviously it wouldn't be anything illegal. *The Woman* was, after all, a lawyer and a State's Attorney at that. Legality aside though, there were things that were bad, immoral, or perhaps dangerous that would still fall inside the letter of the law. The not knowing of it all was what was so brutal.

As the weeks went on though, she began to worry less. She hadn't heard from *The Woman* since the hospital, and as weeks turned into months the anxiety subsided. Eventually, she had days pass without even thinking of her. Soon, days of peace turned into weeks. Now as she walked out of school for a week of teenage frivolity, she realized it had been more than a month since *The Woman*, and her ominous demands, had even crossed her mind.

She still thought of her friends every day, and she visited Mark in the hospital every Saturday night. But the connection between that day and *The Woman* had faded in her consciousness. She was beginning to let herself believe that the day *The Woman* came to collect would never come.

Mica smiled and lifted her face to the warm spring sun. She reveled in the greenery of the returning grass and the leaves budding on the trees. She thought deliciously of a week without worry. She was so intoxicated by the imagined days ahead that she walked right into the hood of a long black Jaguar parked at the end of the circle driveway.

Her hands came down hard on the soft glassy steel of

the car. For a split second she thought she had dented the gorgeous shell of a machine that probably cost more than her dad made in a year. She backed up frantically, her palms up and waving in front of her.

"Oh my God, I'm so sorry," she said, over and over.

The car was running and its windows were up and tinted almost to mirrors. The man in the driver's seat wore a plain black suit with a flat topped cap that suggested to Mica he was most likely a valet and not the owner of the vehicle. He looked up at Mica, squinted slightly and nodded. His door opened and he stepped out of the car. But rather than inspect the spot that still had foggy outlines of Mica's handprints, he stepped back and opened the rear driver's side door.

"Oh, no," Mica said. "I'm sorry for running into you, but I don't need a-"

She was cut off by a sugary voice that poured out of the open door like honey out of a bear shaped bottle.

"It's okay Mica. You can get in. We'll give you a ride home."

Mica felt ice water burn through her veins. A long and agonizing shiver ran down her neck and through her spine. She threw up a little in her mouth. The voice, her voice, felt sticky in her mind, like tree sap you can't wash off your hands. She took another step back, away from the car and swallowed hard, feeling a jagged rock like lump in her throat.

"That's the wrong direction Mica. Come on, it's a beautiful day. We'll take a ride in the country and talk."

It crossed her mind to turn and run, but there was no way she could outrun the car. Instead she just stood there, blankly staring at the open door and trying to will herself to do something.

After a moment, an exasperated sigh rolled out of the dark hole in the car. A pair of long legs in sheer black stockings and slender heels poured out. *The Woman* was dressed different this time. She wore a tight, black dress and long, pearl necklace that wrapped around her neck several times. She had on a large, black, summer hat with a wide, flat brim and wore light pink, glossy lipstick.

"Mica darling," she said in the tone of a mother running out of patience. "As you can see, I have somewhere to be. So if you wouldn't mind, please hop in the car so we can have our chat and I can move on with my day. Otherwise I'll have to have Pete here put you in the car, and then you'll have to figure out some kind of convincing excuse as to why a man was shoving you in the back of a black Jaguar when you get home tonight."

Pete took a step towards Mica and interlaced his fingers before cracking each of his knuckles one at a time. Mica's face went clammy. Her skin felt like a thick rubber mask pulled loosely over her skull, still sagging at the corners. She was shaking and the whole world seemed small and very far away.

The Woman sighed again and shrugged. She nodded towards Mica and Pete gave a crooked smile and took another step towards her. Mica panicked. She took another step back and waved her hands in surrender.

"Okay, okay!" She said.

Pete stopped walking and Mica crept cautiously past him and slid into the back seat of the car.

When she was inside the car the door slammed shut and Pete climbed back behind the wheel. He shut his door and put the car in gear, then they pulled smoothly away from the school. Mica felt trapped. The inside of the car was spacious enough. It was exceedingly luxurious, but it was dark and she felt as though the ceiling was closing in on her.

"How have you been?" *The Woman* asked.

Mica looked back at her bewildered.

"It's been a while," she went on. "It's your senior year right? That's a big deal. Have you had any fun? Made any memories?"

"Just ones I'd like to forget," Mica whispered.

"I see," she said, sadly. "Mica, I'll cut to the chase. I've tried to stay away, to give you space. I know what you went through was difficult and I wanted to give you the time you needed to recover. Both physically and mentally, but I'm in a spot now and I need to call in my condition. I need your help Mica."

Mica stared back in utter astonishment. The Woman spoke so sweetly. She was so sincere. It was the tone of a person who felt terrible about an inconvenience she was imposing. Mica thought it sounded like she really was sorry. She found herself almost feeling bad for her, almost wanting to help her.

"So here's my pickle dear," she said. "I've been in the process of prosecuting this very bad man. He's thirty-six and he raped his son's sixteen year old babysitter. Pretty brutally too. He put her in the hospital for four weeks.

"Thankfully she was able to identify him. He should be going to prison for the rest of his life. But his wife, for reasons I can't begin to fathom, has given him an alibi. That, with the fact that the M.E. found ecstasy in her blood at the time of the rape kit, gave the jury reasonable doubt. They let him off. Scott free. No punishment at all."

Mica was speechless.

"Right," The Woman continued. "So, yeah, this guy is going to walk away after doing this- this- unspeakable thing to this young woman. An act that she is going to cary with her for the rest of her life, and there is nothing I can do about it."

Mica's face was contorted into an expression of panic and confusion.

"So, what do you want me to do?" she asked.

The Woman smiled. She reached down and stuck her hand into her purse. When it came back out she was holding a sleek gleaming handgun. It was almost aerodynamic and smelled of steel and oil. *The Woman* placed it on the seat between Mica and herself.

"Well Mica," she said. "I'd like you to kill him."

The car rolled to a stop in front of Mica's building. Neither Mica nor *The Woman* had said anything since the instructions had been given. They sat next to each other, silent in the weight of the last words spoken. Each of them waiting for the other to speak first. The sun was getting lower in the sky and it shone through the windshield giving the car's interior a strange otherworldly glow that seemed to make the silence even louder. Finally, Mica spoke.

"Ms. Faraday, I don't think I-"

The Woman held up her hand.

"Mica, I wasn't kidding about what I said in the hospital. I will send you to death row. I know that sounds harsh. I know that you can't believe I'd really do it, but I will and I promise you, you don't want to test me."

Mica shook and her eyes began spilling huge tears down her cheeks. She felt all the world rolling over her, pushing her guts up through her chest and out her throat.

"Mica, you were able to do it to my officer. You killed

him with your bare hands. This is a bad man and you don't even have to get close. Ten feet away and you pull a little trigger. You'll barely feel the gun go pop."

Mica shook her head and wiped her face with her open palms.

"That was different," she shouted. "He attacked us. He was going to hurt me, I was defending myself."

The Woman nodded.

"So you say, but it seems unlikely to me that an under-cover police officer would attack a couple of innocent high school kids unprovoked. Either way, it doesn't matter anymore. We're past the time of choices. Now we're in the time of action. There's going to be an action now Mica. Either yours or mine. Either you pick up this gun and so what I've asked you to, or I call my office and we get an arrest warrant issued for you, and you get a needle in your arm."

"That doesn't even make sense," Mica shouted. "You're gonna somehow justify charging me now? After almost a year? And besides, we don't have the death penalty in Illinois, for exactly this kind of reason."

Faraday held a steady gaze. She didn't blink or flinch.

"I'm wondering," she said calmly. "What gave you the impression that it was the courts you had to be afraid of. I said you'd get a needle in your arm, I didn't say anything about the courts putting it there."

Mica was shaking uncontrollably. Her vision was blurry through the onslaught of tears, overflowing out her eyes like a sink left on too long.

"I don't understand," she said. "You're a lawyer, one of the good guys. Why are you asking for this? Why? Why would you want me to-"

The Woman put a hand on Mica's shoulder.

"There are reasons. Maybe they're even good reasons. Maybe they're not. I really couldn't say anymore, but Mica, they're my reasons. For you, the reasons don't matter. What matters to you is that I tell you what to do and you do it."

The Woman's voice was calm, smooth and without any sense of agitation, but it carried a finality as well. There wasn't going to be any arguing. Mica managed to stop crying, but her face was red and swollen and she still felt that crushing pressure in her chest. Her mouth tasted sour and her teeth were covered in a sickening film like she'd been throwing up. She looked at *The Woman*, stared at her with fear and hate as a final sob wrestled its way up her throat.

Mica gave a single nod.

The Woman tapped the headrest on the front seat and the driver opened his door and stepped out. A moment later Mica's door opened. *The Woman* again reached into her bag, this time producing a small flip style cell phone. She held it out to Mica.

"From now on this is the only way you will hear from me. If we ever see each other again it will be because I'm standing across from you asking a jury to put you to death."

Mica grabbed the phone.

"Keep it charged and keep it on," *The Woman* said, like it was a threat.

Mica climbed out of the car and turned to walk away.

"Mica!"

She paused, turned around and saw *The Woman* sitting cross legged in the back of her Jag holding out the small sleek pistol.

"No," she said. "I'm not the bad guy. I don't care what the motives are, this is still bad."

She took a step towards the car, reached her arm out

and slammed the door shut. The driver stared at her for a moment, then climbed back behind the wheel and shut his door. After a moment the car rolled silently away. Mica stuffed the cell phone in her jeans pocket and walked in the front door of her apartment building.

Chapter Thirteen

It was his third slice of pizza and Lt. Don Lorah didn't feel good about it. It wasn't that he felt bad about eating three pieces. The man was six foot five inches tall and built like an Abrams Tank. His fellow officers on the force joked that Angel Armor used Don to protect their bullet proof vests. No, he could eat a pizza and a half and he wouldn't gain or lose a pound. What upset him was that it was gluten free vegan pizza and the principle of the thing turned his stomach.

He hated it. It tasted like cardboard smeared with third tier ketchup and sawdust. He hated it, but he loved his daughter. He'd do anything for her and eating this garbage was one of those things.

"It doesn't matter how big your pecs are dad. Cholesterol can kill you as fast as a bullet," was her favorite mantra.

So now he ate this, and meat free hot dogs, eggless scrambled eggs and drank water instead of Coke. If he could have only one of them back it would be the Coke. A cold CocaCola on a hot day was like tongue kissing the Venus de

Milo. Water tasted like drinking someone else's sweat, but he did it and he didn't complain.

He was eating in his car again. Not his squad car, his personal car. It was becoming a routine for him of late, and he wasn't really sure how much longer it would go on. It couldn't go on forever. His daughter was already asking why he was home late every night. She assumed he had a girlfriend, and no matter how much he denied it, she still kept at it.

"Will you be home on time tonight, or are you having dinner with Claudia again?"

Claudia was today's name. Yesterday it was Phyllis and the day before it had been Amy. Don wasn't sure if she was just teasing him, or honestly trying to deduce who he was spending time with. He just smiled and said he might have to work a little late. The truth was, there was someone, but not a girl.

Scott was the name of the man. Six months ago he had come home drunk from a night out with friends. His wife had been working late at the hospital where she was a nurse. The babysitter, a sweet girl of sixteen, had fallen asleep on the sofa.

Scott came in, and seeing her sleeping, had forced himself on her. When she woke up and tried to resist he punched her in the face breaking her nose and eye socket as well as his own hand. Then he finished himself before climbing off her limp body. He dragged her bloody and unconscious, out of his house and dumped her in the park behind his back yard.

A man walking his dog found her lying in the grass, jeans on the ground and panties torn, he called 911. Twenty minutes later, she was in the ER and Don was walking in to take her statement.

He looked at the young girl lying there in that hospital bed, her face purple and brown and yellow. Tubes running in and out of her in all kinds of places, and thought about his own daughter. He thought about her babysitting for the neighbors, and then friends of the neighbors, and then friends of theirs. He realized at that moment that he let her go into homes of people he didn't know. Strangers' homes, late at night, that this could be his daughter.

He pulled up a chair and sat down next to her. He took her hand in his and held it silently. He sat there with her until her parents arrived and then he sat with them. He sat with them and held their hands and told them that he was going to get the man who did this to her. He promised them that the man would pay. That he would never ever get to do this to anyone else ever again. He promised.

Then he broke that promise. The man's wife somehow alibied him. She said he'd come to have dinner with her at the hospital, that he wasn't home until after the girl was found. She said, with a straight face, that the girl was unreliable and probably had a boy over who did it. It didn't help that the Medical Examiner had found traces of what may or may not have been ecstasy in her blood. Inconclusive evidence, but coupled with the wife's lies and a good lawyer, the man, that filthy vomit bag of a human being, got to walk out of the court a free man. And the poor girl got to live the rest of her life knowing that no one cared what he did to her.

So now Don spent his nights in his car. Sitting outside the man's house. Following him to the grocery store, parent teacher conferences, and far too many strip clubs. He spent his nights making sure that he wasn't hurting other women, other girls. He spent his nights eating vegan pizza in the driver's seat of his car watching the scum of the earth living a life he didn't deserve. He spent his nights keeping his promise.

Tonight had been quiet. The man was at home. The wife was out with the kid. He could see the glow of the television in the family room from the windows. He could see Scott every time he walked across the room to get another beer from the fridge. He was bored, but his anger overwhelmed the boredom and kept him focused.

How long could he keep doing this? How long could he keep his promise to that babysitter who would never be able to trust a man again? He didn't know, but for now the answer was, for tonight.

As the sun crept down behind the houses creating a beautiful orange glow throughout the neighborhood, he saw her. She was walking, coming up the sidewalk in a manner of manufactured casualness. This was something he was used to seeing. People, sometimes even completely innocent people, seemed to feel the need to act overly casual around police officers. They see a cop car and drive one mile an hour under the speed limit. They walk with their hands hanging awkwardly at their sides, or look straight ahead rather than allowing natural head movement. People are always acting that way around him, but this was odd. Odd because he was in his personal car. She shouldn't even know that there was a cop nearby.

He watched the girl walk up the sidewalk and stop in front of Scott's house. She stared at it for a long time. She was young, high school for sure, long red hair tied back in a plain ponytail. She was dressed casually, not trying to impress for sure. Simple bell bottom jeans, tennis shoes, and a t-shirt for a brother/sister rock band that was popular a few years ago. She didn't have a purse on her, or a backpack, which Don thought seemed off for a girl of that age.

After a few moments of staring at the house she walked up to the front door and rang the bell. There was a moment's pause, then the porch light came on and Don could see Scott walking with a slight sway to the door. He opened it and the girl started saying something. Scott stared at her with slight confusion at first, then a smile spread across his face. He shook his head. She said something else and he shook his head again, still smiling with a smarmy expression.

Then this girl, fast as lightning, spun sideways, raised her leg, and kicked the door open with a force that shocked Don to the core. Quickly, he killed the engine and jumped out of the car, but before he could even cross the street the girl had walked into the house and slammed the door behind her.

————————

Mica stood at the end of the sidewalk that led up to the man's house. She stood and stared at it with an empty mind. She wasn't sure what to do next. She wasn't sure because she didn't really know why she was there. The whole mess that led her to this spot, to this nondescript home in a middle class neighborhood, the whole mess was too much for her brain to process.

She took a breath. Then another. Then another. She had to remind herself not to hyperventilate.

He was bad. She told herself that over and over again. He was bad and it was okay for him to pay for what he had done. *The Woman* had sent her pictures, blurry snapshots of court documents that showed the girl's face, her skull, her elbows where she'd been dragged across the pavement.

Mica closed her eyes and saw them. She saw them but

not as they really were. When she saw them she saw Whitney's face. Whitney, her friend whose only crime was being in the wrong place at the wrong time. Whitney, who would never get to go to her senior prom, graduation, college, or wedding, who's whole life was cut short because they had run out of gas.

She opened her eyes and looked at the house. Perhaps this man did deserve to die. Maybe the system had failed that girl and maybe Mica was the only way that those poor parents would have justice. That girl also had her life destroyed by a man. She may not have died, but he still took her life. Mica felt her face harden.

She strode up to the front door of the small home and, once again, paused. This was it. This was the moment that would decide. Either she turned around now, walked back down the path out of the neighborhood, onto the 'L' and back to her own home, or she rang the bell and come what may.

She rang the bell.

For a moment nothing happened. She thought perhaps he wasn't home, or maybe he was asleep. What then? She wasn't leaving and coming back. If she left now it was over. If she walked away she would throw the small flip phone in a public trash can, go home, lock the doors and-

The porch light came on.

Mica looked up just in time to see the door open about half way and a man lean his head out. He was, well, handsome. He was in good shape and wore a fitted t-shirt that let you know he had a flat stomach without being nauseating. His hair was short and well groomed. He had five o'clock shadow, but legitimately, not on purpose. If Mica had seen him on the street she might have given him a second look.

"Can I help you?" he said, with a confused look on his face.

Mica felt a chill run down her spine and it made her shiver all over. She tried to cover it up with a casual smile.

"Maybe," she said. "Are you Scott?"

His eyes narrowed and he gave a subtle glance from side to side.

"Yeah," he said, hesitantly.

"Oh, hi there," Mica said, trying too hard to sound casual. "Um, is your wife home Scott?"

The man hesitated again, then a grin cracked across his face like the plaster of a settling house. He leaned against the door frame in a confident manner and shook his head.

"No, no she's not."

Mica felt her blood go icy and suddenly the man ceased to be anything close to handsome. In that moment his whole being became repugnant and disgusting.

"Is your son here?" she asked, trying to choke back her own vomit.

His smile grew wider and he shook his head again.

"Nope. Just me here. Well, just us I guess."

The world seemed to collapse around Mica and Scott. She felt flames rising up her cheeks setting her scalp on fire. She felt needles pushing out of every pore and acid filling up her mouth. Her breath was hot and acrid and her eyes felt as though they were bulging out of her sockets. Then the tunnel vision collapsed. Scott seemed to be hurtling towards her with that sickening grin smeared across his face. Her body snapped, like a spring coiled too tight.

She didn't think about it. It was complete reflex. Her body pulled into itself and she pivoted, then exploded. Her leg sprang out and she felt the heel of her foot crash into the heavy oak door in front of her. There was the sound of air leaving the man's lungs and the crash of his body hitting the floor behind him while the door crashed into the inside wall.

Mica centered herself. She looked down at the man lying on the floor. He was disoriented, but conscious and regaining his composure quickly. She sensed some other movement around her but pushed it away. She focused on the man like a laser on a sniper's rifle and stepped over the threshold into the house. The man was on his knees now, leaning against the wall, trying to get his eyes to focus. Mica took a quick step forward and threw her fist into his nose.

The cartilage inside his face broke easily under the pressure of her closed hand. His skull, however, was sturdy and hard and she felt the thin bone in her middle finger crack. She winced and turned momentarily to close the front door.

When she turned back the man was on his feet, blood pouring down his face and covering his mouth and chin. He was wobbly on his feet, but his eyes were on fire and his lips were smeared with a ghoulish smile. He laughed and as he did the blood ran from his open mouth and dripped on his shirt and shoes.

"You're a spunky one," he said.

Mica's face contorted into a war like Jack O'lantern that made the man's smarmy smile diminish ever so slightly. She took a step forward and he countered stepping back. She threw a punch, but he flinched and she missed her target. She threw another and he caught it with his left hand.

The man laughed with his whole body.

"Ya know, I teach girls like you. I teach them this. Self defense, down at the gym. You're not bad, not bad at all, but defense is very different from assault."

Mica growled and rushed at him bringing her knee up to meet his groin. He stopped it easily and slipped his arm under her knee bringing it up to his chest. Mica felt herself leave the floor and wriggled violently to break the man's grip, but it was no use. For a moment she thought, *why didn't I just take the gun.*

"I bet you're a black belt," he said, with what sounded like genuine admiration. "First degree right? I'm a third degree myself. Been doing it since I was six years old. You really are good, and very pretty."

Mica shrieked and screamed. She shook and fought and swung her head at him in spastic jabs.

"You're going to be really fun to-"

The front door frame shattered into splinters and the door flew right off its hinges. In the square box of darkness stood a towering creature roaring with anger. The man dropped Mica and she fell flat on the floor slamming her head on the tile. The beast stormed into the room and breathed fire from his eyes. The man screamed, took one step and fell to the floor in a heap. Mica screamed staring up at the gargantuan monster, and then mercifully, the world went black.

Chapter Fourteen

Lt. Lorah looked like a gorilla, and he moved like one too. But not how you'd think. Gorillas, while large, solid, and heavy, actually move with surprising speed when they need to. Don, likewise, sprinted across the street, not even taking the time to close his car door on the way out.

What the hell was that girl thinking? What would motivate a girl of that age to try and attack a grown man?

Don jumped over the curb catching his toe on the edge. He stumbled a moment but caught his footing and dashed up the walk leading to the stoop.

He thought of the girl, the last one. He thought about her lying in that hospital bed. About holding her hand and looking into her swollen eyes. He thought about her parents and making them promises. And about the way they looked at him and pleaded for some kind of understanding. He thought about his own daughter, sweet and kind and always looking to do her part. And again about her walking into strangers' homes. Watching strangers' kids. He saw her face on the girl lying in that hospital bed.

He bounded up the two stairs to the low porch and peered into the front window. He saw the man holding the girl's closed fist in his hand. He saw her pivot and bring her knee up to pound his balls into his throat. Scott blocked her with a simple downward swipe of his open palm. His hand moved under her knee and he lifted her off the floor like a basket of dirty laundry.

The girl squirmed and fought and tried like mad to free herself, but Scott had her and he wasn't going to be letting go. A sickening grin spread across Scott's face like ink soaking into expensive stationary, he was saying something to her.

Don felt like blood was going to burst out his ears. His right hand drew the weapon from his holster on his hip. A scream escaped his throat like water crashing through a broken damn. He stepped back, raised his right foot in the air, and let gravity do its job.

The door blasted open spraying timber pieces all over the room. It flew off its hinges and onto the stairs to the left of the doorway. Don roared as he stepped through the hole in the wall. Both the girl and the man stopped struggling and stared at him.

Scott was in bad shape. Blood was pouring out of his nose and down his face. His shirt was soaked and his face was already starting to swell into shapes that turned Don's stomach. He was breathing hard and smiling that terrible smile while his eyes glowed with hellish intensity.

The girl actually looked okay so far. Clearly she had been a greater threat than Don had given her credit for. A good fighter, but not good enough. Now she was helpless, snared in the man's python like arms.

After a moment of hesitation he dropped the girl hard and stepped backwards to run. The young redhead hit the floor with a thud and Don heard her head crack on the ceramic tile. He raised his service weapon and unloaded the full magazine into the man still facing him.

Scott went down hard. He sprawled out on the floor spilling blood the color of cabernet across the dark white tile. The girl groaned and looked up at Don as he took a slow and hesitant step towards her. Another step and he saw her eyes roll back into her skull. Her head dropped back onto the ground.

Don approached gently. He put two fingers on her neck to check for a pulse. Finding one, he scooped her up and carried her out of the house. He thought about just leaving. Driving away and letting that monster rot on his own foyer floor. Unfortunately, he had shot him with his police issued weapon. Those rounds would be easily identifiable. He couldn't just walk away.

He looked at the sleeping girl in his passenger seat and wondered so many things. Who was she? Why had she come here? He couldn't stand to put her through what was about to happen. She had been like an angel. An angel of death. Sent to put herself in harm's way so that he could do what he needed to, to keep his promises forever. He had to help her, to protect her. Not only from physical danger, but from the trauma of what would come next.

He stared at her for a long time deciding what to do, then he picked up his phone and called his station desk.

Mica woke to the steady rhythm of rain on glass. She was warm and dry, snug in what felt like an easy chair. She wasn't sure where she was or how she had gotten there, but she felt safe. Safe, that is, until she opened her eyes.

Mica jolted up and found herself restrained. Not by the wrists, but a seatbelt strapped across her lap and chest. She was in a car that she didn't recognize and moving fast down the winding ribbon of Lake Shore Drive.

Next to her was an enormous bearded man in a police uniform, but the car wasn't a police cruiser. It was just a regular car. An old car based on the cassette deck in the dashboard. The doors weren't locked and the man wore an unthreatening expression.

"What the fuck is going on?" she shouted at no one in particular. "Where am I? What happened?"

The man turned and looked at her with kind and understanding eyes, then turned back and gazed out the windshield.

Mica reached to unbuckle her seat belt.

"Please don't do that," it was a smoker's voice. "It's raining pretty hard and I'd hate to have anything happen to you if we had an accident."

Mica let her hands fall into her lap, but she shifted in her seat, wedging herself against the passenger door as far from the driver as she could manage.

"Who are you?" She asked.

He turned and looked at her again.

"I'm Lt. Don Lorah, Chicago PD."

Mica squinted and inspected him as they drove through the darkness. The rain was smearing across the windows, making shallow yellow rings from the street lights outside and causing the man's face to bounce between sickly sinister and blackout silhouette. A memory came back and Mica gasped.

"Oh my God!" She choked out. "It's you. You're- You're the beast."

Don turned and looked at her with serious confusion.

"The what?"

"The- The beast. The monster," she said. "You're the one who burst in as I was fighting that man."

Don nodded and chuckled.

"Fighting him? Is that what you were doing?"

Mica grimaced.

"Yes," she said. "I was fighting him."

"It looked to me more like he was swinging you like a nine iron."

Mica relaxed a little. She let herself sink back into the seat and faced forward staring out the windshield.

"He was bleeding wasn't he?" she said under her breath.

Don nodded.

"Yes he was. You must've gotten in a few good licks before he swept you off your feet."

Mica sank a little further in the seat.

"So where are we going now? To the station? Am I under arrest?"

"No," Don said. "You're not under arrest. I'm taking you home."

Mica looked up at him.

"He's not pressing charges?"

Don glared at her.

"What?" she said defensively.

"Young lady, the man you were fighting with is dead."

Mica shot up in her seat again.

"Dead?" she shouted. "I killed him?"

Don glanced over at her and let out a sigh.

"Young lady, what's your name?"

Mica looked suspicious.

"Why?"

"What's your name?" he said louder and with practiced authority.

"Mica," she said. "Mica Kole."

"Mica, Scott, the man that you were assaulting back at that house, he's dead because I killed him. I did so in the line of duty. Protecting you. He's dead because I fired my weapon and what I want now is to know what you were doing there."

Mica stared at him in disbelief.

"I was-"

"Stop," Don inserted. "Mica, it's important that you understand, it's a big deal when an officer fires his weapon. I have a lot of explaining to do now. A lot of paperwork and probably a disciplinary investigation since the target died. I stepped in to help you. To save your life, because the man who you were wrestling with, he would have killed you."

Mica sank back down.

"I stepped up. I stopped him from hurting you. I got you out of there so that you weren't connected to the scene, so you don't have to go through the questions and the investigations. I stepped in to save your life, and now I want some , excuse me, but I want some fucking answers."

Mica started to sob. She crumbled in the front seat of Don's car and let all her pieces fall apart. She cried and cried and when there were no more tears to cry, she dry heaved into her hands. Don watched her with sympathetic eyes and undying patience. When Mica finished, when she coughed her last cough and gulped in a long and cleansing breath, Don put his hand on her shoulder and spoke.

"Why were you there Mica?"

She closed her eyes and allowed herself to swim in the darkness for a while. She felt the heavy hand resting reassuringly on her shoulder. She heard the prattle of heavy rain on the windows and steel roof of the car, and the ferocious whoosh of passing vehicles. She held her breath. She squeezed her fists and slowly she composed herself and began to think.

It surprised her when her first thoughts were not of the dead man lying alone on the tile floor of his own home. They weren't of the creature slash savior that had dragged her out of there lucky to be alive. No, her first thoughts were of her parents, at home in their warm kitchen, probably cooking the night's supper. She imagined heavy, savory aromas filling the air and soft incandescent lighting wrapping everything in a comfortable Hallmark glow.

She thought of them and what they thought of her. Their sweet, perfect, overachieving daughter who always did the right thing and tried so hard to please them. Where did they think she was right now? Could they even imagine it? What would they think if they knew what had happened? If they knew about that day with Whitney and Mark, what happened with *The Woman* in the hospital, in the car. If they knew what had happened in a stranger's home tonight. If they knew what was happening right goddamn now.

Her breath got choppy again and she squeezed her eyelids together even tighter. She felt the last vestiges of her tears press out the corners of her eyes like the final drops of juice from a well pressed grape, ready to become wine.

Finally she let her mind turn to the events of the evening. She replayed the walk from the L stop to the brownstone. She lingered in the memory of standing on the sidewalk deciding her future. With trepidation, she eased into her recollection of ringing the doorbell, and...

And that was it. That's all she could remember with any

clarity. She tried to skirt around the edges of the encounter. Tried to peer in and grab glimpses of the fists and bruises and blood, but all she could see was that smirk. That sick oily smile that made her feel like he was going to eat her for dinner and lick the juices from his fingertips. That picture floated in her consciousness and burned her eyes behind her closed lids. It burned them. She could actually feel them burning, then-

The face was gone and in its place was The Beast. The Monster that blew down the door like The Big Bad Wolf, roared, shot fire from its eyes, and felled the man with the sound of thunder. His eyes, fierce but kind, faded into view through the fog of silhouette and looked at Mica with an expression of understanding and compassion.

Mica rubbed her eyes with her thumbs and let out a long and stuttered sigh, then opened them and looked up at the man that saved her life.

"You won't believe me," she said softly with a grave tone that carried the weight of her fear.

"Why don't you try me?" Don said.

Mica turned in her seat.

"I'm going to. I'll tell you. I'm just warning you now, you aren't going to believe it."

And she did.

And he didn't.

"Do you know her?" That's what he kept asking. "The other girl. The one who- the one he attacked. Do you know her? Is she a friend of yours?"

She kept shaking her head.

"No. I've told you a dozen times now. I don't know her. I've never met her. I don't live around here. I don't go to her school."

He looked at her skeptically, and rephrased the question.

"Maybe at a party? An event outside of school? Maybe a friend of a friend?"

Mica slumped in the seat.

"Officer..."

"Lorah. Lieutenant Lorah," he corrected.

She sighed.

"Lieutenant, I promise you, I've never met that poor girl. It's awful what happened to her, but I promise, I swear to god and all things holy that I do not know her. Not at all."

Don let out a long breath and rubbed his eyes with the palms of his hands.

"Mica, I'm trying my best to understand what's going on. You show up at this guy's house. A guy who just recently was acquitted of a serious physical assault on a young woman close to your age. You claim you've never met the man or had any interaction with him or anyone who has. You ring his bell, and then without provocation you attack him with, as far as I can tell, the intent to kill him."

He glanced at Mica and she nodded silently.

"But he's never done anything to you."

"That's right."

"Or anyone you know."

"Correct."

"Okay, but you know what he did? You were familiar with him and what he's been accused of. Familiar before you visited him."

"I've read about it," Mica said in an exhausted voice.

"Right, but you don't know her. The other girl. The one he assaulted. You've never even met her."

"Right."

Don ran his fingers through his hair and gripped and pulled at the muscles in the back of his neck.

"So what? Was it like, I don't know, the principle of the thing? Just righting a wrong that society let slide? 'Cause I gotta say Mica, you don't look like the vigilante type. No cape. No cowl."

Mica stared out her rain streaked window and felt herself giving up.

"Lieutenant, I told you what happened. I told you, you weren't going to believe me, but I told you anyway."

Don took a breath to speak, but Mica didn't let him get a word in.

"I appreciate what you did for me tonight. I don't think I've said that yet. Thank you. Thank you so much for being there, for not leaving me to die. Thank you for risking your own life and your career to save my life. Thank you for getting me out of there so I don't have to face whatever it is that's coming next. Seriously, with all my heart, thank you."

Mica turned and looked him right in the eyes.

"But Don, I've told you why I was there and who sent me, and there's nothing else I can say or do to help you understand. You don't have to believe me. I can't make you. I didn't expect you to in the first place, but my story isn't changing. I have no more evidence to persuade you, so, unfortunately we are at the point where you either have to arrest me, or you need to take me home."

Don stared at her with frustration. Her story was crazy and she knew it. She said he wouldn't believe it and she was right. There was a time, maybe, maybe that he would have considered it, but that was a long time ago, back when he was a rookie.

He had to admit that her story had stayed consistent. The entire time he made her retell it, over and over. Front to back, then back to front. Questioning her about different parts of the tale, out of order, hopping around, trying to trip her up. Through all of it she hadn't faltered, but that didn't mean it was true, only that she knew the story very well.

She had details, but everyone knows the details are the most important part of a convincing story. If you're going to lie about something make sure you have details. Tiny insignificant bits that lend weight to the bigger claims. Remember a wristwatch, or a strange pair of glasses. A kid on a bike or a dog that wouldn't stop barking. Details sell the story, and of those, she had plenty.

Also, her story was thorough. She didn't skip steps or hop around in time. She knew everything that happened from that first day of school, when the incident had supposedly happened, until this afternoon when he dragged her unconscious out of the house. There was a logical narrative that, other than being bat shit crazy, made a kind of awful sense.

Still, it wasn't true. It couldn't be. Fifteen years ago, sure, something like that could have happened. Hell, something like that had happened. Something exactly like that. He had seen it, met the people involved, but he had also seen it end. He had seen the bodies of the State's Attorney and the FBI woman. He had watched, with the rest of the city, as the investigation into the SA's corruption had revealed everything from bribery to murder, and he had seen the city clean up its act and move on from the black eye the whole thing had left them with. But even then, even when things like what she was describing had actually happened, even then it wouldn't have involved a seventeen year old high school student. Even then that would have been preposterous.

Sure she was stubborn, and sure she was sticking to her

story, but she was lying and he knew that if he grilled her long enough she would break. She would crack open and spill out. The truth would come pouring out of her like water from a shattered vase and she wouldn't be able to stop it anymore than you could catch the water with your bare hands.

The question now, the question he rolled around his head like a steel ball in a maze was, should he? That was the dilemma. Should he push this poor girl. Should he keep rolling her, keep pressing until he squeezed out what he wanted to hear. Was it worth damaging her more than she already would be from this encounter? Was it worth the chance that she could end up really broken just to satisfy his own curiosity?

Because that's what it came down to, it was his own personal interest he needed satisfying. He had already removed her from the scene. Already covered up her involvement in the death of Scott the rapist. He could no more bring her in now than he could put the bullets that were resting in Scott's chest back into his gun.

Her answers to his questions were not for the official record. They wouldn't appear on any report or be entered as testimony in any investigation. He had taken on the full burden of that terrible man's untimely end, and he had done it to save this girl. To spare her from further suffering. So why was he pushing her, pressing her, making her suffer at his hands?

He let out a long disheartened breath and turned away from her. He put the car in gear and pulled off the shoulder of the road and back into traffic.

"Tell me where you live," he said.

Mica turned forward and gave him her address. She leaned her head against the cold glass of the window and stared out at the slick asphalt as it slipped by under the tires of the car.

At her house he stopped in the street without pulling to the curb. They sat silently for a moment, then Mica opened the door.

"Mica," Don said sadly.

She turned and looked at him. He slipped his fingers into the breast pocket of his uniform and produced a small white card.

"If you change your mind, if you decide you want to talk, give me a call. I'm here to help you. Really. I'm here to help."

She took the card.

"No offense Lieutenant, but I kinda hope I never see you again."

She climbed out of the car and slammed the door shut. Don watched her walk slowly and casually through the rain to her front door, then disappear into the soft yellow light of her home.

"I'm sure you do," he said to the empty car. "But I have a feeling we will see each other again soon."

He was right. It only took one day.

Chapter Fifteen

It was still raining the next morning when Mica's mother came to wake her up. She was lying in bed listening to the heavy drops cascading off the flat roof of her building. She was warm and cozy, stuffed in her bed under her lavender comforter with Mozart's *The Magic Flute* playing softly out of the speaker on her clock radio. Her mom tapped lightly three times on her bedroom door before opening it a crack and poking her head into the room.

"Darling, are you awake?" she asked, in a soft early morning tone.

Mica rolled over under her enormous bedding and looked at her mother.

"Yeah mom, I'm awake. Just enjoying the Sunday rain."

Her mother paused and listened, gazing dreamily off into space.

"You do have the best room for it," she said. "It's so loud in here."

Mica smiled.

"Do you need me to get up for something?"

Her mom snapped back into the present and put on a serious face.

"Well, I don't," she said. "But your teacher's here. He's downstairs. He said you're late for a student government meeting. They've been trying to reach you all morning. They were starting to get worried."

Mica frowned and wrinkled her nose up into an impossible knot.

"What?" she said, confused. "I don't have anything today. What teacher is it?"

Her mother opened her door the rest of the way and stepped into the doorway. She leaned casually against the frame as if settling in for a long conversation.

"Um, Mr. Cataldo I think he said."

Mica's frown shifted, but didn't leave her face.

"Yeah, Pete Cataldo. He said your partner has been waiting for you down at the-"

Mica jumped out of bed.

"He's HERE?" she shouted frantically.

"Well, yeah," her mother said, sounding confused by her daughter's sudden change in attitude. "He said he was going to give you a ride to the school."

Mica was pacing back and forth now on her bedroom carpet, staring at the floor.

"Is everything okay?" her mother asked, beginning to sound concerned.

Mica looked up at her with panic painted on her face. She put her arms up as if to say 'how should I know?' Then sat down on the edge of her bed and leaned her elbows on her knees. She hung her head between her legs, then sat bolt upright and stared daggers at her mom.

"Tell him I can't go. Tell him I'm sick. I don't feel well. Tell him I'm sorry, but I can't get out of bed."

Mica's mom gave her a disappointed stare.

"Mica, come on," she reprimanded. "This isn't like you. It sounds like people are counting on you. You can't let your partner down. This stuff is important. Why don't you get dressed, go with Mr. Cataldo, get done what you need to get done, then come home and we'll watch an old black and white movie together."

Mica gazed at her, trying to come up with a better excuse, then she felt the warm water of acceptance rush over her and she dropped her shoulders and let out a long breath.

"Okay," she said. "Let him know I'll be right down."

Her mother smiled sweetly at her.

"I'm so proud of you," she said.

Mica rolled her eyes and whispered, "You shouldn't be," under her breath.

Twenty minutes later Mica was sitting in the backseat of Autumn's black Jaguar, being driven by 'Mr. Pete Caltado' to the downtown offices of the city's State's Attorney. He was chatting away at her, but she had mostly tuned him out. She was dumbfounded at the gall to send Pete to pick her up at her parent's house. It was a ballsy move, and clearly intended to show her that she wasn't afraid to do whatever it took to keep Mica in line.

"I said, I'm surprised your parent's went for the teacher story. They saw me pull up in the Jag. Are they just the oblivious type?"

Mica snapped out of it for a moment and looked at Pete in the rearview mirror.

"I go to a really good school," Mica said. "They probably just assumed you were one of the poor teachers."

Pete blew a breath out through his teeth.

"Okay, princess."

"Fuck off," Mica whispered.

"What?"

Mica squinted into Pete's eyes in the mirror then slumped down in her seat and let herself drift off into thought. When she came out of it again they were in the parking garage at the Daley Center. Pete stepped out of the car and opened Mica's door. She stepped out and was greeted by another man.

He was taller, chiseled face with slicked back jet black hair and a well manicured beard. He wore a nice suit, but it was clearly off the rack and didn't fit right in the sleeves or chest. He was polished and professional and very very serious.

"Mica Kole?" he said.

"Obviously," she replied with a tone of exhaustion.

"Very good," he said. "I'm Chris Marshall. I'm S.A. Faraday's assistant."

Mica chuckled.

"Of course," she said. "Always two there are. No more. No less. A master and an apprentice."

Chris looked at her confused.

"Take me to The Emperor," she said.

It was a long elevator ride and a quick stroll through beige carpeted hallways and past glass walled offices. Finally they arrived at a small waiting area just outside two large maple doors.

"Have a seat," Chris said, nodding at a set of overstuffed chairs against the far wall. "Let me make sure she's ready for you."

Chris disappeared through the huge doors and then reappeared moments later. He waved at Mica and told her that S.A. Faraday would see her now.

Mica stood and shuffled slowly past reception and into

the dragon's lair. Inside she found a vast space filled with every cliche ever put into a lawyer movie or TV show. There was the large, ornately carved desk with the huge high backed leather chair complete with brass tacks. Two slightly smaller chairs sat opposite the desk. There was a small conference table with ergonomically designed chairs around it. There was a large flat panel TV hanging above, what had to be a fake fireplace. There were floor to ceiling bookshelves on two walls, all filled with the kinds of volumes you see on lawyers' bookshelves in television commercials. The office gave a vibe that felt more like theatre than law.

The Woman was sitting in the ridiculous throne behind the desk watching Mica as she took it all in. Mica walked up to the desk and stood in silent attention waiting for instructions to sit. None came.

"Well, you kinda fucked that up last night, didn't you?" was the first thing *The Woman* said.

Mica sat without an invitation.

"It got done."

She was nervous, terrified actually, but she was determined not to let this woman control her, not her feelings, not her mind. She could control her actions, she had that power, but she would not let her break her. Not her spirit.

The door to the office opened and Chris stepped back in the room.

"Ms. Faraday, Lieutenant Lorah is here."

The Woman smiled. Mica went white.

"Send him in," she said and looked back at Mica. "Well, now that we have both halves of the dynamic duo here we can figure out exactly what went wrong."

Mica's mouth went dry and she heard the door open and close again. *The Woman* stood up and ran her hands over her suit, then held out her right hand for a handshake. The Beast's huge paw slid into her delicate palm and *The Woman* sat back down.

"You are in some serious trouble Lieutenant," she said.

There was a pause, then the same deep growl that Mica woke up to after the encounter at the house.

"Yes Ma'am," it said.

"Do you have an explanation as to why you emptied your weapon into an innocent man?"

Mica listened to the silence and took a breath to speak, but was cut off by *The Woman*.

"What I want to know Lieutenant Lorah is, were you there watching Mr. Craig, or were you there following the girl?"

There was a pause, then Don, sounding confused said, "I'm sorry Ma'am, I'm not sure I know what you're talking about."

The Woman laughed and looked over at Mica. There was a moment and then Don's towering frame came into Mica's view. He looked down at her and his whole face went white as a ghost.

"You two are like the fucking Keystone Cops, ya know that?" *The Woman* said.

"Mica, what are you-"

He stopped himself and the switches all turned to the on position.

"You were telling the truth."

Mica nodded.

"You need to be more trusting Lieutenant," *The Woman* said.

He looked back at her with fire in his eyes.

"You bitch. You psycho bitch. You're going to prison for this you crazy monster."

The Woman just smiled.

"You're right of course. Mica fucked up pretty badly despite my easy to follow instructions. The whole thing was a disaster and I most certainly would have been finished, but then you stepped in and fixed it all for me."

Don gazed at her, stupefied.

"You stepped in and fixed the whole thing Lieutenant. You emptied your gun into an unarmed man and then you cleared the crime scene of the only evidence that you were defending a poor innocent girl. Now the whole incident is on you. You are the one who's going to go to prison Don. Your career is over and you are going to spend the rest of your life face to face with the trash that you spent your career putting away."

Mica was sobbing now. Long heavy tears streaked across her face leaving itchy salt on her porcelain skin. She shook and convulsed and choked on her own breath.

Don stared at *The Woman*, then at Mica. His face went from angry to afraid, to defeated before his body crumpled and he fell into the chair next to Mica.

"You two made a mess the likes of which I could never have imagined." *The Woman* said. "But I have a way out. Since I am in the unique position to clear up the matter and make all of this trouble go away, I have options for the both of you."

Don and Mica both looked up at *The Woman* who was now standing behind her desk, holding court and conducting the two of them as if they were musicians in an orchestra.

"Mica, you are not done here. Not by a long shot, and lucky for you, I have your next assignment right here."

She tapped a cream colored file folder sitting on the center of her desk.

"I'll be sending this with you when you leave. You'll have two days to complete it or you'll be spending some quality time with Chris out there, and let me tell you, is he ever eager to please me. He goes above and beyond in everything he's tasked with."

Mica looked into her lap.

"Lieutenant, you have a bit of a choice to make."

Don glared at her.

"You can get up and walk out now, and I'll be forced to issue a warrant for your arrest. You'll be tried and convicted of Mr. Craig's murder and spend the rest of your life in prison.

"How would your daughters feel about that? How would your little girls handle their daddy going to prison? Going to prison for murder? How would your teenager feel? Your baby? What's the little one's name? Elle? You don't want little Elle growing up without her father do you? Or-"

"Or," he growled back.

"Or, you can help out Miss Kole here. Make sure she's safe and that the job get's done. You can keep an eye on her. Think of it as a protection detail. Advise her on strategy and make sure nothing bad happens. You do that and I'll clean up the Scott Craig mess."

Don stood up suddenly and paced the space behind Mica's chair.

"I make sure she stays safe, make sure nothing happens to her, and you take care of the rest?"

"That's right," *The Woman* said.

"What's the job?" he asked.

The Woman handed him the folder and he flipped through it. He glanced down at Mica a few times and frowned, then handed the folder back to *The Woman*.

"Yeah, okay," he whispered.

The Woman smiled.

"Good. Well, that's it. Two days."

Don nodded, looked down at Mica pityingly, then turned and stormed out of the office.

"You can go now too," *The Woman* said, turning her attention to Mica.

Mica stood hesitantly and looked around the room. *The Woman* lifted the file off her desk again and held it out for Mica to take. She stared at it for a long time, then took it out of her hand.

"It's going to be okay Mica," she said.

Mica looked at her, feeling sick and frightened.

"I promise, it's going to get easier. It's going to be alright."

Mica turned without a word and walked out of *The Woman's* office feeling more broken than she thought possible.

Part Three

Elle

Chapter Sixteen

The question hangs there in the air. It's quiet and uncomfortable and no one seems to want to be the first to speak. After a couple moments I can't remember if they're waiting for me to talk or not. Finally I take a breath.

"I think-"

"Maybe you shouldn't," Elle says flatly.

I look up and meet her eyes. She looks at me cold, stoic, and unfriendly.

"Shouldn't what?" I ask.

"Think."

"Elle," Allie cuts in.

"No Allie," she says. "I'm serious. If I was you Mal, I wouldn't think about anything. It seems to me that your fucking thinking is what got us into this fucking situation in the first place. Maybe thinking isn't your strong suit."

I let out a deep breath.

"I need to talk to Mica," I say.

Elle lets out a laugh like a bomb going off.

"You most certainly do not," she says, with a forcefulness I've never heard from her before.

"Elle," Allie starts again, but again Elle cuts her off at the knees.

"No way Allie. No way! We just got out from under that bitch."

"Does it feel like you're out?" Allie asks bluntly.

Elle stares at her, anger smoldering in her eyes.

"She burned down our home," Elle says, the forcefulness having left her voice. Now she sounds pleading, vulnerable, frightened even. "She sent people to our home to kill us. More than that. To kill everyone. She's mad at Mal so she tries to kill innocent people."

"What?" I say. "What are you talking about Elle?"

"They blew up our building Mal. Our building. We're not the only ones who lost everything. I can't believe I have to remind you of that. Other people could have died. Other people lost their homes."

She was getting frantic again.

"You may have been the target Mal, but what they did, how they did it, they could have killed a lot of people."

"That's true," I admit, and suddenly there's something needling around in my brain. I'm not sure what it is, but there's something that itches. Something that feels wrong. Something about what Elle said makes me feel, somehow off. I start rolling it over, trying to isolate it. "That's true," I say again.

"I'm still not so certain it actually was Mica though," Allie says.

"Seriously Allie?" Elle says baffled. "After everything you've told me about Mica and what she's done. What she's had you do," she says throwing an open hand in my direction. "All of that and now you're saying she isn't responsible for this?"

Allie has an apologetic look on her face.

"So what then? If it's not Mica then who? Who Goddammit? Com-Ed? Did you forget to pay the fucking electric bill Mal?"

"Elle," I say, but she won't hear it.

"No. Oh my God no! No to both of you. I can't take this anymore. You're both hopeless. I don't know if you're delusional or just stupid, but I can't do this. I- I just can't-"

Elle is standing now, pacing the room and dragging her nails through her long auburn hair like stone plows through spring soil. Her eyes are frantic and her body is shaking.

"I forbid it!" She shouts at me. "Do you hear me? I fucking forbid it. I should be divorcing you right now. Fuck! I'm a prosecutor, I should be turning you into the police right now."

She stops moving and plants herself in the middle of the room. She takes a deep breath and lowers her voice to a soft growl.

"I love you, for fuck knows why, but I do. So I'm not leaving you, and I'm not turning you in. Yet. I'm giving you a chance to make this right. To fix this and fix our lives, but that chance is predicated on you never ever, fucking ever, seeing Mica again."

She stops. She gulps down air and lets her body relax a little. She looks, for a moment, like one of those plastic and string figures that collapses when you squeeze the base.

Allie and I sit motionless staring at the wild eyed creature standing in front of us. Elle straightens herself up, smooths out her hair and finds a way to center herself. She cocks her head and puts on a shallow plastic smile.

"Do I make myself clear?"

Allie and I nod without making a sound.

"Good," Elle says. "Now, if you'll excuse me, I need to go get some fucking Xanax."

Elle turns, runs her hands over her suit, rolls her shoulders slightly, cracks her neck and walks out the door. A moment later we hear her car start in the driveway and disappear down the road.

Allie and I are still sitting motionless and silent in her living room.

"Malcolm," she says finally.

"Yeah," I say without looking at her.

"You need to go see Mica right away."

"Yeah."

"Right away!"

"Yeah."

Elle drove with intensity. Her foot lay like a stone on the gas pedal and her arms jerked wildly at the steering wheel and gear shift lever. The car cut through the city on diagonal streets then wound around its edge on the long waterfront drive. She kept the speed up and took every shortcut available to move herself towards her goal.

And what was that goal? Well right now she wasn't entirely sure. Her world was in shambles. Her marriage, such as it was, was a mess. Her job was probably over, and there was a good chance her life itself was in jeopardy. The solution, at this point, was unclear. Even trying to think about it made her slip into an anxious sweat. Ultimately she didn't see any way of closing this business.

Malcolm, the police, they both thought that the explosion at their building had been intended to kill. Malcolm saw himself as the target of a savage mob boss determined to end him for trying to get out of the organization. The cops thought it was Malcolm trying to, who knows what, destroy evidence? Their line of thinking wasn't clear, but what else could you expect from suburban cops that never had to look into anything more complicated than a stolen ten speed bicycle. Perhaps they thought he was trying to kill her.

"Ha!" She laughed out loud.

That was absurd. Malcolm may have been a killer, but he was no murderer and the distinction was as wide as an ocean. He could no more have killed Elle than he could have sucked his own cock, and despite her personal feelings on the matter, she had made many efforts to assure he'd never have to even think of trying that.

The idea that the explosion was intended to kill him was equally absurd to her, but she was a prosecutor and trained to look at things differently. If it had been city cops, city detectives investigating the explosion, they would have been able to tell right away that the bombing was a message, not an actual attempt. People with the cunning and ability to set off a bomb like that, they don't make mistakes. They knew that Malcolm wasn't in the building when they set it off. They knew he was out, but nearby. They knew he would see it.

All that aside though, this was not the time to come up with answers or plan for the future. Right now her focus wasn't on trying to solve the *who done it*. She had her own notion of who was behind it, but that didn't matter now either. No, what she needed now was comfort. Comfort and protection. What she needed now was home.

She swung the wheel hard and the car shrieked and fishtailed onto a narrow street just a few blocks from the nicer of the two ballparks in the city. It was dark and cars lined both sides of the street. She gunned the engine and let her German luxury car sail over the speed bumps in the road, then swung it again pointing the nose down an ancient concrete alley that was mostly crumbled to gravel now and slammed on the brakes. She sat, the car still running between two medium sized apartment buildings, and let herself breathe. She closed her eyes, pictured a warm quiet place. A place of safety and comfort. A place where she could cry, scream, let out all her anger and frustration. A place to collect herself and find the strength she would need to take the next steps.

She looked out the passenger window at the red brick wall of her father's building. She imagined his kitchen, all amber in the soft incandescent glow of forty watt light bulbs. She imagined the comforting smell of something in the oven and a glass of plummy red wine in her hand. The reassuring feeling of her father's large hands on her shoulders and his deep voice telling her it would all be okay.

She cut the engine and stepped out of the car, composed herself and walked around the building to the front door. This building, like every other one on the block, had four floors and a sub-level. Each floor had two flats, except the sub-level which had three studios. Next to the front door was a row of eleven small black buttons, each with a small white card next to it with a name scribbled in handwritten blue ink. She scanned through them, found the button labeled 'D. Lorah' and pressed it.

Chapter Seventeen

I sit silently at the bar sipping a neat bourbon and spinning my wedding ring on my finger. It's an aimless habit and I think most men do it. Most married men, when they have something troubling on their minds. I have such troubling things. Things that are hanging on me, gnawing at me, drowning me in angst and unrest.

Two days ago I had a job. It was a bad job and I didn't like it. I didn't like what it made me do and I didn't like how it made me feel. I didn't like the person I had to be when I did it, but it was a job. I imagine that a lot of folks, regular people I mean, I imagine they don't all like their jobs either. So I try to keep a little perspective on the matter. I had a shitty job but it came with financial security, stability and personal safety. I also had a dead sexy wife who was successful, independent, and for reasons I could never understand, crazy about me. Things were okay. Not perfect mind you, but okay.

But now, here I am, drinking at a bar I've already been kicked out of once this week, waiting for a person who may or may not want me dead, and being investigated by the cops for a crime that I, legitimately, did not commit. Sure, I may be responsible for it tangentially speaking, but I didn't actually do the thing, ya know.

And the worst part of it is, I'd love to shake my head and act shocked that this is happening, but I can't do that. I know the score, and if I had two working brain cells I could have seen it coming. I knew when I walked in that morning that no one quit Mica. No one did that job then just left and went on with their lives. I knew it then, so I can't act surprised now.

But that's the rub. I do feel surprised. Something about the way Mica let me go that day, the way she looked at me, I really thought that was it. I really thought I was out.

Then the bomb. Something sits wrong with me about that too. Something about what Elle said. It could have killed a lot of people. Even if I was the target, it could have killed more people. Innocent people. That wasn't Mica's style.

My jobs are always laid out very specifically. The details worked out for me, timelines, locations, even methods. Always planned with the lowest impact on the outside world. Never a witness to silence or an innocent bystander hurt. Never a single piece of collateral damage. Never once a person hurt that wasn't the intended target. Never a person who didn't have it coming.

But that's not true. The Phillips kid. My last job. Elle had said he was a witness. He hadn't done anything wrong. He was a witness to his sister's attack and he was going to testify against the assailant. Mica had sent me after an innocent kid. That wasn't like her, just like the bomb.

I've used a lot of methods to kill a lot of people. I'm not proud of that, and if I could change my life and take it all back I would. If I could go back to that moment, when I was nineteen, and let that disgusting shit-sack in the tower of roaches kill me dead, I would take that chance in a heartbeat. I'm not proud of the things I've done. I justify it by telling myself that these things need doing, but deep down I know it's not true. I know that killing a bad guy is exactly the same as killing a good one. I know the games we play to convince ourselves otherwise are just that, games. I know it's all crap and that I'm no better than a toilet. That said, in all the years and all the times I've killed, I've never killed with a bomb.

I've shot people with all manner of guns. I've stabbed and cut men and women. I've smothered and strangled and poisoned adults, and even teenagers, and when the situation called for it, I've beaten men to death with my bare hands. But I've never, not ever, blown someone up. Neither has anyone else working for Mica as far as I know. I've never really given it much thought until now, but when I think about it, it's true. I've never been asked to use an explosive of any kind before and it seems so clear why.

Bombs are messy and they attract attention. Gunfire is loud, people notice it, but they run away from it. No one hears shots fired and runs to see what's happening. An explosion though, when people hear that bang and see that fireball, they all come sprinting to see what's burning.

Worse than the attention though is the mess. You never know what's going to happen with a bomb. You have to be far away when it goes off. Far enough, at least, that you don't go up with it. Distance robs you of control. You can't control who you hit. You never know who's going to be walking by when it's time to set the damn thing off. You don't know if your target is going to be with somebody else. It's true for cars, offices, houses, and especially apartments.

Mica would not have set a bomb. Mica would not have

risked hurting others, and Mica would not have sent me after that Phillips kid. Not on purpose. Not knowing who he was. That's two events in two days. Two times that someone has died or almost died under circumstances outside of Mica's M.O. I'm starting to understand that these two things are connected, just not the way I originally thought. Unfortunately, the only person who can confirm it is unavailable at the moment.

I feel a light hand on my shoulder and I jump.

"Whoa there tiger," Mica's soft voice says.

I turn and see her back in her usual uniform. Barefoot, in soft denim bell bottom jeans and a loose fitting cotton shirt that's hanging off one shoulder.

"Didn't I already kick you out of here once this week? And didn't I bail your ass out of jail just today and tell you to get the fuck out of Dodge? You're not good at following instructions Malcolm."

I lean back in my bar stool and take the rest of my drink in one swallow.

"Who is Kelly Phillips?" I ask, dryly.

Mica's face hardens and her body stiffens up. She leans back against the stool behind her and lets out a long sigh.

"Shit," she whispers.

I nod and she pulls herself up on the stool and leans in towards me.

"Mal," she says, seriously. "Do you have a smoke?"

Chapter Eighteen

Her father's home was nice, but not what she'd grown up in. She was eight when her parents had split up and her dad had moved out of their home and into a small studio apartment. Elle could remember those days, the tension in the home and the endless fighting. Her mother had said terrible things about him after that. Awful things that Elle had never believed.

Her father had always tried to be a good man. He had never known his father. The old man had left him and his mother when he was only three years old. His mother had to work two or sometimes three jobs just to keep them fed and clothed. Her dad had vowed, from childhood, that he would do better. That he would help people and take care of his family at any cost.

After high school he passed up football scholarships so that he could go to the Police Academy. He had dreams of working his way up in the force to a position of leadership so that he could change the organization. He wanted to make it more focused on serving the people and helping the communities. All he ever wanted was to make the world a better place. It was ironic, she thought, that helping someone out, someone who couldn't help themselves, was how it all fell apart for him.

She remembered that night, how he wept and how her mother shouted. She remembered her mom's anger when he left the force, and her furry when she found out what he was doing, and who he was doing it for. She remembered how she called him a coward and a fraud and forbid him to see his own daughters. It wasn't until much later, when she learned the whole truth, that she understood and saw her father for real for the first time.

Her dad walked into the room carrying a tray with two glasses of red wine and a plate of Triscuts and soft cheese. He set it down on a low coffee table in front of her and handed her one of the glasses. She smiled softly in appreciation and took it, setting aside her small clutch purse.

He lifted a glass for himself and walked across the room to a high backed leather chair and sank himself into it, like an old habit. They sat like that for a while, silently sipping their wine and inspecting each other as if from a long absence. Elle shifted in her seat and pulled her legs up on the sofa.

"It's good to see you sweetheart," her dad said, finally.

Elle looked him in the eyes, then diverted her attention to the floor.

"Yeah, I miss you dad."

"I miss you too," he said. "But coming here is a bad idea. You know that. What if she found out? What if- what if Mal found out? How would you explain that?"

Elle was already nodding her head.

"I know," she said. "I know, I know, but-"

He stared at her with sympathy and understanding, but

with an undertone of disapproval that only a parent knows how to weave in.

"I didn't know where else to go. I don't know what to do. Everything's gone to shit and I don't see any way out of it."

Her father nodded his head and sipped his wine. There was another pregnant pause before he leaned back in his chair.

"What happened with the bomb?" he asked.

Elle straightened up and put her feet back on the floor. She set her glass down and picked up her purse. She stood and began pacing the room, her finger absently rubbing at the gold clasp fastener on the clutch. Her father set his glass down as well and folded his hands in his lap.

"That's what I'm saying," Elle said, harsher than she intended to. "I don't know."

"That was supposed to be a contingency, a last resort," he said, exactly like a father reprimanding a daughter.

"I know dad!" She snapped. "You're not hearing me. It wasn't me! I didn't do it!"

He leaned forward with a frown.

"You didn't set it off?"

"That's what I've been trying to say."

Don tilted his head in thought.

"Was it an accident?"

Elle shook her's in the negative.

"No! It was called in. Called in on a cell spoofing Mal's signal."

"But who else knew it was there? You didn't tell anyone you planted it? Who even knew it existed?"

Elle was still shaking her head.

"That's just it dad. No one. Who would I tell? It's just me, you, and her."

Don let out a long sigh. He wiped his face with his palms and put his hands on the arms of the chair.

"So, then... you think it's her? You think she was trying to kill him?"

Elle shook her head.

"No. No dad, she doesn't make mistakes. If she wanted him dead, he'd be dead. She never misses."

"So?" he said, drawing out the vowel.

"So, I think it was her, but I think it was a message. I think it was a message for me."

Don squirmed. "You think she want's you to kill him? That doesn't sound right. She's never asked you to do anything like that before, has she?"

Elle shook her head.

"No, not Mal. Well, not just Mal. I think she wants the whole thing shut down. The whole group. I think she's closing up shop."

"You mean-"

Elle nodded.

"Did she actually tell you this?"

Elle sat back down. She was rigid, nervous, her knees pressed tightly together and her hands white knuckled around her small purse.

"A long time ago," she said. "Before Mal, before anything really. Well, anything involving me. Sometime in high school I think. She didn't say anything explicitly, but she told me a story. It was weird and I didn't really understand it at the time, but it stuck with me. Then later on, when she brought me into the, well, whatever, sometimes I'd think about it and it started to make a little more sense. It wasn't until yesterday that I really understood though."

Elle lowered her head and went quiet. She was very still.

"This story," Don said. "It was about you killing Mica?"

Elle looked up at her dad with tears in her eyes. She shook her head.

"No," she said.

The gun went off and the small blue clutch fell to the floor open. She felt the recoil move up through her wrists and elbows and disperse into her shoulders and back. The acrid smell of gunpowder filled the space and her father fell forward out of the blood soaked chair and onto the floor.

Elle wept. She sat on the sofa sobbing. Feeling the sharp pains of shame and regret stabbing at her heart and lungs. She wept until her eyes burned and her bones ached. Then she wiped the tears from her face and the prints from the gun.

She laid the small revolver on the floor next to her father's body, then took out her phone and opened the camera. She sent a text message, then she walked out the front door of the building, into her car, and drove away towards the lights of the city.

Chapter Nineteen

It was three o'clock in the morning when her car pulled off the street into the abandoned lot. The rain had stopped a few hours earlier, but it was still eighty-five degrees outside and it left the air feeling like soup. There was no moon, and the floodlights outside the restaurant had been turned off after closing, leaving the woodsy parking lot feeling more like a clearing in some ancient Asian forest.

She stepped out of her car slowly. One foot on the wet pavement, then a considerable pause before the next. She stood up and leaned against her car for a moment before closing the door softly and making her way through the muggy early morning air. She wasn't being especially cautious, though she was a cautious person. There was no need for additional care here. This was a safe place. Safe like home is safe. Safe like family.

She wasn't moving slowly out of fear, or prudence, but out of sheer exhaustion. It had been a long night. A night of physically and emotionally draining work. Her job was hard and it took a lot out of her, leaving her body aching and her mind foggy. Normally she would go home, climb into bed and let the sweet tide of sleep ease her muscles and cool her brain. She would wake up in the morning refreshed and ready for the new day's challenges, but tonight she couldn't. Tonight she had to deliver something to her boss. Something that, she felt, couldn't wait.

She cut through the thick swampy air, feeling sweaty and sticky. At the huge double doors she dug in her pockets and found her key. It was heavy and ornate and, frankly, a pain in the ass to have to carry. She stuck it in the brass plated keyhole and give a firm turn to the left. A heavy leadened clunk came from inside the thick wood door and the slab of mahogany released and hung loose in front of her. She grabbed hold of the black cast iron handle and swung the considerable door open.

The first thing she noticed was that the alarm was not set. There was no bothersome chirping asking for her to enter a four digit alarm code. She took a moment to compose herself, wiping sweat from her forehead and running her fingers through her long dark hair. She rolled her neck and shoulders and let her body crack and pop and straighten out. She rubbed her face and eyes and took a long deep cleansing breath. She licked her thumb and wiped a smudge of blood from the pinkie fingernail of her left hand. That's when she noticed the second thing.

The lights were on. Normally at this time everyone was gone and the place was silent and dark, but no, the lights were on and she could hear muffled voices. Over at the bar there was a young woman sitting alone. She was pretty, pale, and young, with unsettling blue hair like the sky over the sea before a storm. She was poised, sitting on her stool with perfect posture and sipping a dark red wine from an over-sized glass. She was distinct, the kind of person you wouldn't forget, which was disturbing because she felt like she'd seen her before.

After a moment of slogging through the cloudy archives of her memory she gave up and set herself back to her task at hand. She reached into her jacket pocket and pulled out a flat black leather wallet. She opened it and stared at its contents, then snapped it shut and made a B-line to the back room where Mica would be. As she pushed through the beaded curtain that hung between the dining room and Mica's office two things happened. First, she heard the sound of something scraping across the tile floor on the other side of the restaurant, and second, Mica's eyes went wide as saucers.

In the room were four people. Mica stood behind her floor level desk looking shocked and even a little frightened. Across from her was Don, her bodyguard, and two women she'd never seen before, or wait, maybe she had.

One she was sure she didn't know. She was fit but curvy with dark black hair. She stood in the back of the room, mostly in the shadows. The other felt familiar, tall and slender, she wore a narrow black skirt and white blouse with white vertical stripes. Her hair was dark brown and fell preternaturally across her shoulders and perfectly framed a set of horn-rimmed glasses. She was confident looking, powerful even, and deeply unnerving. The gears in her mind churned and turned looking for the connection, and then-

"Oh, Kelly, what are you doing here?" Mica stammered. "This is, uh-"

Her memory went click.

"Faraday?" Kelly said confused. "State's Attorney Faraday?"

Mica went white.

The woman glared at Kelly.

"Nice to make your acquaintance," Faraday said.

Kelly felt a hand on her shoulder and another grabbed the wallet from her right hand. She spun to see the blue haired girl standing behind her.

"That's Lexi, my personal assistant," S.A. Faraday said by way of introduction.

Kelly took another step into the room and Mica gave a slight shake of her head. It was a gesture that made Kelly's already palpable anxiety worsen by a matter of degrees.

The blue haired girl handed the wallet to Faraday who opened it and gave a whistle of surprise.

"Very nice work, uh, Kelly is it? Very nice indeed. I'm impressed, especially given that I specifically asked that this job be handled by Mr. Karma."

Kelly looked at Mica. She stared back with wide eyes that betrayed a sense of fear Kelly had never seen in her boss.

"I do kind of wish you hadn't found this though," Faraday said, tossing the wallet onto Mica's desk. It landed open displaying a flat gold shield adorned with an eagle and a blue and white identification card.

"You're just supposed to put them down, not take their tags."

Kelly's mind started working. Pulling in blood and adrenaline that cleared the fog and brought sharpness of attention. She wasn't supposed to be here. Not tonight. She wasn't supposed to see this meeting. This group of people, meeting in this place, there was something wrong here, something off.

She inched closer to Mica and examined the room anew. The Faraday woman stood across from them dressed like you'd expect a State's Attorney to be. Behind her, the dark haired woman she didn't recognize. She looked to be in the same basic uniform as Faraday. To her right, the blue haired Lexi with a silver ring in her lip. Her right hand stuffed unnaturally in the pocket of her leather jacket. To her left was Don wearing the same black suit they all wore. His hands were stuffed casually in his pants pockets and his jacket was open letting his Beretta hang out in his shoulder holster. He looked calm and stern. The stoic picture of power without an ounce of fear.

Mica was afraid though, and that terrified Kelly. It was wrong. Kelly had never seen Mica look frightened before. Not ever. And why would she? Everyone feared and respected Mica. Mica was a badass, and on top of that, she had Don. Don would never let-

Kelly froze. She looked over the room again. She was on one side with Mica. On the other side, Faraday, the mystery woman, the Lexi girl, and...

Kelly stepped closer to Mica. Now they were shoulder to shoulder.

"Why did you come here Kelly?" Mica said softly.

Kelly didn't say anything.

Faraday took a step closer.

"Because she thought you'd want to know that the person you sent her to kill tonight was an agent with the F.B.I."

No one moved.

"She thought that because, she didn't know that you already knew it. Right Kelly?"

Kelly turned and looked at Mica dumbstruck.

Mica stared back at Faraday with a cold expression of pure hate.

"It's easier, we've found," Faraday said, "to get you all to do what we ask, if you think you're the good guys."

Kelly stepped away from Mica.

"Kelly, I'm-"

Kelly waved her off.

"If it helps any, in the big picture, you really are. I assure you. You just can't see the whole picture."

Kelly choked on her breath and backed up.

"So we have a little problem here," Faraday continued. "I needed to get this agent out of the way. Really, he was becoming a nuisance. Big picture here, remember. It was Mica's job to get that done. It's always been Mica's job to get that done. It's always been Mica's job. I don't much care how she does it. If she want's to bring in you grunts to go out and do the dirty work, that's her prerogative, but ultimately it's her job. That's our arrangement. Mica's job, Mica's responsibility, and Mica's secret."

Kelly stuffed her hands in her jacket pockets and backed herself against the wall.

"But now there's you," the Faraday woman said. "Now you know too, and you know what they say about two people keeping a secret?"

Kelly nodded.

Chapter Twenty

"My lawyer's in the car," I say as we walk through the kitchen to the back door of the restaurant.

Mica laughs at this. She runs her fingers through her long red hair revealing individual strands of gray hiding under the surface, and shakes it out like a movie star.

"Are you considering legal action against me, Malcolm?"

"No," I say. "I'm just letting you know that she knows where I am and who I'm seeing. If I was to disappear or anything, ya know."

She pushes open the emergency exit which swings wide without a sound, despite multiple signs warning that an alarm will go off. She leads us out to an open air garden, walled in by a huge cedar fence. Its small, with four raised garden plots crisscrossed by paths of black river stone. Over the paths are wires dangling Chinese lanterns glowing dimly, red and yellow. Mica walks us to the back corner and sits on the low garden wall under a flaming red Japanese maple tree. She gestures for me to join her and I do.

"Got that smoke?" she asks.

I reach into my coat and produce a pack of Pall Malls and a lighter. She takes them and lights up immediately, pulls a deep drag and holds it in for a long time before releasing the cloud of silver smoke into the air.

We sit together silently for what seems like ages. We share a glance here and there, spend some time staring at our shoes and Mica smokes the cigarette I gave her down to the filter. When she finally squeezes the dim cherry off the butt and into the stones at our feet she turns and looks at me sadly.

"Malcolm, who do you think I am?"

I'm taken aback by the question. It's shocking to me in a way I wouldn't have expected. It's a question I've asked myself a million times, and in all those times I've never come to a satisfactory answer.

There are stories obviously. It's a question everyone asks and everyone has their theory. It's like asking who killed JFK. Some people think the answer is obvious, and others are less convinced.

Mica Kole, sure, did you know she's the great-great-granddaughter of Al Capone? No, I heard she's a disgruntled former director of the F.B.I. Nope, she's more than that, she's the immortal personification of the wrath of God. The Old Testament God. The God of the Hebrews, sent to punish the world for its sins.

You hear these things. All of them, I swear. You hear them in crack dens, and whore houses, and tent cities on Lower Wacker Drive. You hear them, but you don't really believe them. At least I don't. To me, all Mica has ever been is a boss. She's the only authority figure I ever took seriously in my whole life because she's the only person I was ever, actually afraid of.

Parents, teachers, even the cops, they couldn't really

hurt you. Not really. But Mica, I never doubted for a second that she would kill me dead if I ever crossed her even once.

I lean forward, my elbows on my knees with my hands clasped between them and I sigh.

"I don't know. Honestly, I have no idea. I think I have less of an idea now than I did before, which trust me, wasn't much. You could be anyone, any one of the things they say about you. None of them would surprise me. Hell, I'd probably be least surprised of all, if you did turn out to be the actual fucking Angel of Death."

To this Mica nearly chokes on her own laughter. She turns to face me, crossing one ankle under the other, looks straight into my eyes and suddenly relaxes. Her shoulders drop and her hands fall into her lap. She looks more human than I've ever seen her. She could be anyone. Just a woman you pass on the street. She could be someones's sister. Suddenly she looks young and beautiful and vulnerable.

"That one's my favorite too," she says.

I wince. Seeing her this way has the exact opposite effect I would have thought. It makes me nervous, uneasy. It puts me on guard. It's as if the ground I thought was solid rock just turned into paper thin ice and I'm terrified that if I move, I'll fall through and drown in dark arctic water.

"I am, in fact, not the arm of the lord," she says, with an air of disappointment. "I am, at best, the left toe of Saint Jude."

I frown.

"I'm sorry, I'm not- well, I'm not anything I guess. I've never been to church."

She smiles sadly.

"I'm nobody Mal. I'm middle management in a company that doesn't exist. I'm a slave to an idea that wandered off its path a long time ago, and I can't do anything about it. I can't quit because if I do, all the people that I'm protecting will be punished for it. All the people I care about will die."

I turn to face her holding my breath, waiting for the right words to come to me. I loosen my tie and undo the top button of my shirt. I run my fingers through my hair and bite my lower lip.

"Mica, who's-"

"Kelly Phillips?"

I nod.

Mica lets out a long and tired sigh.

"Kelly was like you. She was one of my soldiers. Like you, she had a troubled youth and like you, one of my people found her and brought her into the fold."

I notice my mouth is hanging open and quickly close it.

Mica nods.

"She did the same kinds of jobs you did. There's more of you than you know Mal."

"And you-"

Mica shakes her head.

"I didn't," she says. "And therein lies the problem."

My brow wrinkles and I shift my weight.

"I love you guys," she says, wistfully. "You don't know it, but I do. It's why I put the money aside for each of you. I want each and every one of you to reach the point where you can't stand what you're doing anymore. Where each of you comes to me and demands out. When you become the kind of person who knows that this is wrong and wants a life that's right."

My brain somersaults in my skull. I'm lost. I stand up and begin pacing back and forth in front of her, trying to find my center of gravity.

"The problem is, I'm not in charge. That's what you have to understand Mal. I'm a pawn on the board, not the queen, and the person moving all the pieces, she doesn't care about anyone."

I stop and look at her, panic painted on my face.

"What do you mean you're not in charge? Who is? Who's running this shit show?"

"I can't tell you that Mal. For your own safety, I can't tell you that."

I laugh.

"My safety? Are you fucking kidding me?"

"Mal-"

"And Kelly? Is that what happened to her?"

Mica doesn't move.

"What, did Kelly figure it out? Did she get a glimpse behind the curtain? And then what? You had her killed for that?"

"No!" She shouts. "No, it wasn't me! That's what I'm trying to tell you Mal. The person above me made that happen."

"But it was you that sent me after her brother. You sent me to kill an innocent man."

Mica looks at her feet, then up into my eyes.

"Yes," she says.

"I just don't understand," I say. "How did this happen? I mean how did you get here? I mean, Jesus. Who could get to you like that? Yeah! Wait! How did it happen? Why didn't you just send Don to fix..."

I trail off.

Mica stares up at me.

"Don doesn't work for you."

She nods.

"Don doesn't protect you, he watches you. He's not a bodyguard, he's a babysitter."

She stares back blankly.

I walk over and sit back down next to her.

"Well, you have me," I say. "And who else? How many more? Let's get them. Let's get them all and let's go after whoever it is that's controlling you. Why don't we tear the whole thing down?"

Mica gives me the same sad smile.

"I don't know who I can trust Mal. Until someone wants out, like you did, until they say they don't want any part of this anymore, they may as well work for her."

I look up.

"Her?"

Mica shrugs.

"*The Woman*. That's what I call her."

I gaze at her.

"Kelly wanted out?"

She smiles.

"I don't know. I think so. I think she had figured it out. She came to see me, but she walked in on a meeting. Once she knew for sure, once *The Woman* knew she knew, there was no way she was going to get out of it alive. She tried. She shot up the place something terrible, managed to get out of here, but-"

"They follower her," I say.

she nods.

"Found her at her brother's place. She was packing a bag. They beat her so bad Malcolm. They beat her just about to death. Then her brother walked in. They emptied a magazine at him but somehow he got away. That's when she called me and told me to have you take him out."

I reach out and put a hand on her shoulder.

"You can trust me," I say. "Me and Elle, and I've got a very strange but also very sharp woman in my car that wants to help us."

She shakes her head.

"There's nothing to be done Mal. You just need to leave. Leave your car here and run. Just run as fast and as far as you can. If you can get out of the country, that would be even better. Just you. Just you Mal. I made my bed a long time ago and now it looks like it's time for me to lie down in it."

I stand up and look down at the broken soul of the woman I used to work for. Suddenly I feel a sense of strength wash over me and I straighten up with an eagerness of purpose.

"No," I say.

She looks up at me.

"Nope, sorry. I don't work for you anymore. You don't give me orders. Now, I'm going to figure out who is behind this and I'm going to put a stop to it. It would be considerably easier if you were with me on this, but with or without you I'm not going anywhere until the whole fucking thing is a burning pile of rubble at my feet."

"Or you're dead," she offered, helpfully.

"Yeah, that's right," I say, my confidence faltering for just a moment. "Or until I'm dead."

She looks at me with pity, then slowly, it melts away and the steely eyed resolve that I'm used to seeing on my boss returns. She stands up and puts a hand on my shoulder. There's a long silence between us.

"Then we need to go see Alex," she says.

When I climb back in the car, Allie is relaxed in the passenger seat, sipping a coffee from a thermal mug. She has the radio playing music that was popular twenty years ago and looks to me like she doesn't have a care in the world.

I shut the door and say, "Hey."

"Hey," she says back, nonchalantly. "How'd-"

The back driver's side door opens and Mica climbs in. She shuts the door and buckles her seat belt.

"All set," she says.

Allie sprays coffee across my windshield. She coughs, chokes almost, and turns around in her seat. She gapes at Mica, then turns and stares at me.

"Allie," I say. "I'd like you to meet Mica Kole."

Allie freezes. Slowly her face melts into the warmest of smiles. She turns back to face Mica again and extends her hand over the seat.

"So very nice to make your acquaintance."

Mica smiles and shakes her hand.

"Absolutely. My pleasure entirely Allie. I've heard so many nice things about you."

"Oh stop it," Allie says charmingly. "You're making me blush."

After she waves off Mica's compliment she turns back to face me.

"Malcolm, would it be possible to speak to you outside for a moment?"

I sigh and she mouths the word 'outside'.

I roll my eyes and open the car door. Allie steps out and quickly starts walking away from the car. After a few strides she stops and looks back at me. She waves her hand beckoning me to follow her.

I stick my head back in the car.

"Sorry Mica, I'll be right back."

"Take your time," she says.

I close the door and follow Allie into the dark. After a few more paces she stops and smiles at me.

"Yes?" I say.

"Hey," she says, in a chipper voice. "How'd the meeting go?"

"Alright. I think we've got a plan now at least. We've got to get some supplies, but then we're going after the ringleader of this whole shit show. This is all such a mess, and I know that none of it will hold up in court so don't even remind me of that little nugget, but the legal battle is going to have to be a separate thing.

"Ultimately, I didn't do what they are charging me for, but proving that may require me to face up to the things I did do. I don't really know how you're going to defend me against that, but we'll cross that bridge when we come to it. My main focus now is tearing down this whole messed up organization."

Allie's nodding.

"That's great. Good to hear," she's saying, in a sing song voice that suggests she's not really listening. "Quick question. Are you fucking insane?"

"It's okay Allie," I reassure her. "Mica is with us on this. She's a victim here too. Just like I was, she's under someone else's thumb. She's not the one pulling the strings, never has been. This whole time she's just a pawn, like me.

Allie stares at me with a dumb look on her face.

"Oh my God Malcolm."

I let out a sigh.

"Do you think I'm fucking stupid?" she says. "I know that. I know there are people above her. That's people by the way Malcolm. Not one person. People is plural. That's my point. You can't trust her because you have no idea if she's acting on her own motives, or the motives of the people controlling her."

I grunt and throw up my hands.

"I don't know anything Allie. Shit. I only just met you today, but you're here with me too. I've got nothing left Allie. Nothing left to lose. I'm trusting you, and I'm trusting her too. So you can come and be a part of it, or you can walk out now, but either way I'm going back to the car and I'm going to put an end to this fucking insanity. Now. Fucking tonight."

Allie stares at me for a moment, then shrugs, smiles again and starts walking back to the car. I stand motionless watching her leave again. Finally she shouts back over her shoulder without stopping.

"Okay. Jesus Mal, are you coming?"

When we get back to the car Mica is wiping coffee off the window and dashboard with old Taco Bell napkins I keep in my glovebox. She steps out of the car and gives us a timid smile.

"Everything okay?"

"Oh sure," Allie says. "Just a little lawyer, client chat. You know how it is."

Mica looks unconvinced.

"Oh, one thing though," Allie adds. "If you do decide to betray us, could you try to just kill him? I've got a brunch on Sunday I can't miss, and so much stuff to do next week."

Mica looks at Allie like a crazy person and mutters, "Uh, yeah. Sure. No problem."

"Phew, thanks so much," Allie says with exaggerated gratitude.

We all climb back in the car and I rev up the engine to go.

"Alex won't be at his office at this time of night," Mica

says. "We're going to have to go to his house. I don't have a way to contact him there, so you might want to let me be the one to knock on the front door."

"That's fine," I say. "But I want to swing by the motel first and get Elle-"

I'm interrupted by both of the women in my car shouting, "No!"

Chapter Twenty-One

There was a list. Seven addresses in and around the city. Elle got it in a text message while they were at Allie's place, just before they found Malcolm playing with those stupid puppies. That's all it was, seven addresses. There were no names attached, no explicit instructions spelled out. Just a list of seven addresses from an unknown cellphone.

Elle knew what it meant. She didn't need to have it explained. She knew what it was even before she started reading it, and she knew what she was supposed to do. These were the addresses of the people in S.A. Faraday's organization. These were the people that Elle was to eliminate tonight.

"In eight hundred feet, stay straight onto Sheridan Road," the vaguely feminine voice of Elle's GPS said.

She was on her way to the third address on the list. A house in Roger's Park on the far north side of the city. She didn't know who lived there, or how they were connected to Faraday, but she knew they were on the list and it was her job to make them gone.

Two of the addresses she did know. The first one was hers. It was the apartment that she had shared with Malcolm. It was gone now, blown to pieces by a bomb she set, but someone else detonated. That explosion, that night, that was the beginning of the end. That was when the pieces of this whole charade started to fall apart.

She was pretty sure that the explosion was a message, not a mistake. It was intended to tell her that it was time to start cleaning things up. Things had gotten sloppy and mistakes were being made in the outer echelons of the group. People putting things together that they shouldn't, including her husband. He had begun to figure out that he wasn't doing what he thought he was. At least not always, and he was beginning to suspect that he might not be doing it for the person he thought he was.

He was getting suspicious and he was getting brave. Brave enough that he walked into Mica's office and quit. People didn't do that. Faraday had worked very hard over the years to make sure the people Mica brought in believed that she was a monster, and that they could never get out alive. For the most part Mica let that impression stand. She let Faraday run her exactly the way she ran her soldiers, but what Mica couldn't do was follow through.

It had been a problem with her from the very beginning. It's the reason Elle's dad had gotten sucked into the group in the first place. When push came to shove, Mica couldn't pull the trigger. So when her people came to her, when Malcolm came to her and wanted out, she let him go. She let him walk away to start a new life.

That's why they blew up her building. Faraday wanted to let Elle know that enough was enough. It was time to end it. It was time to get rid of all the deadwood and start over from scratch. She was telling Elle it was time to kill Malcolm.

The list confirmed this. There it was, right at the top of the list, their apartment. It was gone now, but the message was the same. She had to kill Mal. He was first on the list.

First on the list, but he'd be the last one she took care of that night. She needed time to prepare herself for that job. Malcolm may have been a killer, but she wasn't. Not by vocation at least.

Her role in the organization had been administrative, so to speak. Intelligence perhaps. Her job was to keep track of Malcolm, to know his every move and every thought. Her job was to be his wife.

The truth was that she'd actually grown rather fond of him over the years. At first, when S.A. Faraday had told her that she wanted her to keep close tabs on him, she had been fine with it. But when that became dating him, and then marrying him, well she was less agreeable to that. Marrying a man just to spy on him seemed disturbing, disgusting even.

Letting him touch her, letting him kiss her, letting him fuck her, that wasn't a reasonable ask. But Faraday wasn't reasonable. She was single minded and determined, and she demanded the same of her people, and Malcolm was charming. He was very charming in fact, and within a few weeks of sharing a bed with him, on not so subtle threats of death or worse from her boss, she found that she was warming to the guy. By the end of their first year together she had found that she genuinely liked him.

She would never go so far as to say she loved him. That was a bridge too far. She liked him and didn't mind role playing house with him, and fucking him when she had to.

It was better than a bullet, so she found she could even enjoy that, or at least she could fool herself into thinking she could.

Still, he was a co-worker and nothing more. They served the same agenda and had the same boss, even if Malcolm didn't know it.

The second address on the list is where she'd just been. It was her father's apartment. Her dad had worked for Faraday for as long as she could remember, and though he had expressly forbidden it, she knew from an early age that she would too. She was brought up to be in Autumn's army, the pavement being laid from her childhood.

That Faraday Woman, as her mother had always caller her, had begun contacting Elle secretly when she was only ten years old. By then her parents had already split up and her mother had made it clear that it was almost entirely because of Faraday, or rather her father's inability to put his wife and family before Faraday and her mission. She's why he quit the police force. She's why they lost their health insurance and pension. She's why he was always working late and coming home stressed. She's why her dad cried at night, alone in the dark when he thought everyone else was asleep.

Elle knew now, with thirty years of hindsight, that it wasn't that her father chose Faraday over them, it was that he never had the choice in the first place. He could either do what he was told, go where she told him, scare who she told him, and kill who she told him, or not only would she kill him, but the woman he loved and his daughters too. Her father let his wife, whom he loved dearly, leave him and take his daughters to save their lives.

The other five addresses were anyone's guess. They could be five more soldiers like Malcolm, or other kinds of service providers. One of them could be Faraday's attendant Lexi Lefevre, the blue haired ice queen that was never far from Faraday's side. She would be a challenge. She was smart and strong. She had cunning, problem solving skills, and an athleticism that surprised most people. On the surface she was Faraday's porter, but the general belief was that she was more like a bodyguard and that she was not a person to be trifled with.

One of the addresses was probably Mica Kole herself. Elle wasn't sure she'd ever been to Mica's actual home. In fact if you had asked her a few hours ago she would have said she assumed Mica lived at the restaurant. But now, well, it only made sense that one of these was her home. If Faraday's intention really was to gut the entire operation and start over, Mica would have to go too.

Of course Elle had no way of knowing for certain that's what was happening. She had never been told it was, nor had she been asked. It was just an assumption. An assumption based on a story. A story she'd heard twenty-five years ago when she was a junior in high school. Elle was captain of her school debate team. It was an honor that she'd worked hard to achieve and she was exceedingly proud of it. She wasn't in athletics, but she bought a Letterman's jacket anyway so that she could display the big 'G' that stood for the school's name and the pin that indicated that she was a captain.

Debate in school is different than most people think. You aren't casually arguing a notion back and forth with a snarky opponent. It's not like the presidential debates you see on television. You have to talk fast, auctioneer fast, Micro-Machines guy fast. You have to talk fast and you have to list facts. It's a crazy skill set to master and she was just that, a master. She worked with her club and held coaching sessions every day after school, but the truth was, the rest of her team members were average at best.

She was leaving a competition in the suburbs one weekend when she ran into That Faraday Woman in the parking lot. This happened a lot. Faraday would just show up places and pull Elle aside for a little chat. Life lessons, like she was some sexy Yoda. It happened frequently enough that Elle had stopped being surprised by it.

"Elle," The Faraday Woman shouted, from a row over in the parking lot.

Elle looked up and let out a short breath.

"Ms. Faraday. Hi there. What are you doing here?"

Faraday walked over to Elle's car and leaned over the roof in a casual manner and smiled.

"I came to see you speak. You're good."

Elle smiled shyly and said, "Thank you."

"No, I mean it," Faraday gushed. "You're really good. Your teammates a little less so, but you are exceptional. You should go into law."

Elle blushed.

"Really though, that team of yours needs... well it needs something."

"I know," Elle said.

Faraday shifted positions and gave a wry smile.

"Can I tell you a story Elle?"

Elle looked at her watch then shrugged and shut her car door. She leaned against the car as well and looked across the roof at The Faraday Woman.

Faraday took a breath.

"So, there was this sailor. I say sailor, but really he was a pirate. Ya know, Jack Sparrow type. Back in the time of the East India Company. So he was a pirate, but not the captain. He was first mate and he worked really hard and followed all the orders the captain gave, but eventually it wasn't enough for him.

"Now pirates, they don't have a lot of upward mobility as it were. You pretty much live and die for your captain and that's the most you're ever going to have, but this fellow, we'll call him Michael, he just couldn't settle for that. So one day Michael goes into the captain's quarters and blows his head off with an old ball and powder pistol.

"Ya see, he just up and kills the captain of the ship. He then marches all of the other crew onto the deck and tells them what he's done and informs them that he's the captain now. But ya know what he does now?"

Elle stares for a moment, confused by where this is going, then shakes her head.

"Right, so the new captain, our guy Michael, he gives the crew members a choice. They can stay and work for him, or they can get off at the next port and go their separate ways. He gives them a choice. So, ya know, most of them stay, but a few of them decide they want to leave. So a day or so later they arrive at some port in the Caribbean and the one's who chose to leave, they get off the boat and walk away."

Elle looks surprised.

"Not what you thought would happen right?"

"No, not at all," Elle said.

"So," Faraday continues. "The next day the ship sets sail with the remaining crew. When they get out to sea Captain Michael calls the crew out on deck and thanks them for choosing to stay with him. He then takes out his scabbard and kills each and every one of them and throws their bodies overboard.

"They all died, except, in point of fact, one of them. He spared a single ship's mate. A thirteen year old boy. He said, 'you're young and know not what loyalty means yet, but I will let you live and you will be my first mate, and together we'll sail these seas and I will teach you what it is to be a man'."

Elle looked stunned.

Faraday smiled.

"And?" Elle asked.

"And? And they did. They sailed together for years and years and built a new crew and the boy was his first mate."

Elle frowned.

"Anyway," Faraday said. "Good performance today. Just gotta do something with the rest of the team."

Faraday patted the roof of the car and turned and walked away. Elle was profoundly confused. She didn't understand what the point of the story was. She couldn't fire any of the kids from the team, and she wasn't going to kill anyone. It was one of those stories, one of those moments that are so baffling that you may never understand them, but you never forget them either.

It haunted Elle for years, that story. She would think of it at the strangest times, and never at any point did she understand what it meant, until now.

It meant it was time to kill the crew. It meant that no one who knows where power comes from can respect that power for very long. It meant that when people start to understand how, or why, the Captain is captain, then it's time to get rid of that crew and find a new one.

It meant that Elle was the child and it was her job to clean house and then she would take her place as second in command. She wouldn't have to live with a man she didn't love or work a job she wasn't passionate about. It meant that her's would be the name that was feared and respected.

Elle pulled into the driveway of a small brick townhome. She popped open her glove box and pulled out a small pink SCCY CPX-2 9mm pistol. She pressed the release and slid out the magazine. She counted ten rounds and slid it back up into the grip, pulled back the slide, chambered a round and climbed out of the car.

Chapter Twenty-Two

It's a hard conversation to follow. Both women talking at the same time. Talking over each other sometimes and finishing each other's sentences at others. The details are all smeared and overlapping, but the broad strokes are that Elle is not who I think she is.

"Don't you think it's odd Mal?" Mica asks. "Strange I mean, that you never met her parents?"

"That's not strange. They passed away before we met," I say. "A house fire in the suburbs."

"No, they didn't actually," Allie says.

"What do you mean they didn't?"

"They're not dead. Look Mal-"

"No, you look! I've been married to this woman for five years. We love each other. We're going to start a family. We share everything. We share a bed. We share our whole lives! We-"

"And when did you share what you actually do for Mica?" Allie asks.

I stare back. I feel anger burning in my chest. My

fingers curl into tight fists and I feel my nails digging into my palms.

"Well?" she says.

"You know when," I growl. "You were there."

"Exactly," Allie says. "You think you have a monopoly on secrets? You think only you could be that sly? Malcolm, you just told her today, but she's known the truth all along. She's known since the day you met her. She's actually known longer than that."

I stare back blankly and feel the anger turning into nausea.

"It's true," Mica says.

I turn and meet her eyes.

"Wait,"

Mica looks back at me with sad eyes.

"Are you saying Elle works for you?"

I turn back and look at Allie again.

"Does she? Does my wife work for her?"

Allie shakes her head.

"No," Mica says. "Elle doesn't work for me. She works for my boss."

"Here we go again," I sigh. "Ya know Mica, if we're gonna work together on this, you're going to have to let me in. I'm gonna need to know who we're fighting. Who you work for. Who's running all this? Who does my wife work for."

Mica stares back at me. She looks frightened and unsure.

"Mica, I need to-"

"Faraday," Allie interrupts.

Mica's face goes white as death. Her eyes dilate and she jerks to look at Allie.

"How'd you-" she starts.

"She works for Autumn Faraday, Mal. Mica, Don, your wife. They all work for the Cook County State's Attorney. Do you get it? Do you understand how big this is? Do you see why we have to be so careful?"

I choke a little on my own spit and gape at Mica. She gives a sad nod and turns to look out the window.

I look back at Allie.

"How do you-"

"Jesus Mal, I tap your phones. How do you think I beat your wife in court so Goddamn always? She's a good lawyer Mal. I tap your phones. All of them. Your cell, Elle's cell, your home phone. Everything, well, except her office because it turns out it's hard to get an illegal phone tap on a government phone line."

I feel like I'm drowning.

"Mal," Mica says, without moving.

"Yeah," I say.

"One more thing."

I sigh.

"Somehow I doubt that very much."

Mica looks at Allie who nods her approval.

"Elle's not the person you thought she was, not just because of who she works for and what she does. She's actually not the person you thought. Her maiden name. It's not Smith or Miller or Jones or whatever it was she told you. Your wife's name is Lorah. She's Elle Lorah. Your wife is Don's daughter."

Chapter Twenty-Three

The red door swung open and Elle stepped out of the house onto the small cement stoop. Her heart was pounding and the night air felt cool and refreshing. She took a long deep breath and focused on the starry sky above her. Her body was high as a paper kite from all the adrenaline and she needed to come down before she made her next decision.

She saw it all the time in court. Over and over, criminals that might have gotten away with it, but for making bad choices in the heat of the moment. Detailed plans that got changed mid execution because of emotions or a foggy mind. They'd get sloppy and make mistakes that got them caught. Mistakes that they could have avoided if they had just taken a moment to regroup and calm down.

She walked back to her car and climbed into the driver's seat. She took a pack of tissues out of the center console and wiped the tiny droplets of blood off her face. She looked at the tissue getting damp and red and felt the panic swell up, then pass, and her heart began to slow.

There had been two of them in the house. An attractive

man in his early thirties wearing an expensive looking gray suit, and a girl, mid to late twenties, wearing brand name workout clothes. They were in the kitchen eating some kind of takeout off the granite countertop and sipping a pale yellow wine. They both looked up in confusion when Elle walked in the room. Then, quickly, the girl's expression changed to fear while the man's changed to anger.

Elle didn't know which one was the target, but since they were both there they both had to go. Which to do first posed itself as a question for a split second before the answer shouted itself in her face. The man would be a tougher fight if it came to blows. Better to risk a tussle with his partner than have to go hand to hand with him.

She raised her little pink pistol and put a quick bullet through his windpipe. He dropped to the ground and blood sprayed in heavy streams across the counter, cabinets, and hardwood floor. Elle quickly re-aimed and put another 9mm round through the side of his head. His body went still and Elle turned her attention to the girl.

She was screaming and tears had already run her mascara halfway down her tan cheeks. Elle raised the gun and without pausing to aim squeezed the trigger twice. The glass cabinet door behind the girl shattered and sprayed shards of frosted glass and an assortment of herbs and spices across the room.

The girl bolted, charging towards Elle, looking as if she was going to shoulder check her on the left. Elle knew she was trying to make it to the door down the hall, and she wasn't going to let it happen.

She tracked her movement down the sight of the gun, and just as the girl closed in on five feet from Elle, she pulled the trigger. The body dropped like a stone and sprayed blood across Elle's face and clothes. On the floor it gushed crimson across Elle's feet, soaking into her shoes and between her toes. She lowered the gun and used her left thumb to wipe the liquid off her eyes.

Now she was using Kleenex to get the sticky stuff off her hands. She picked up her phone to see what was next on the list when the screen lit up and the caller I.D. said 'Malcolm'.

"Hello," she said, after swiping the green answer button across the screen. "No, I'm not ready to talk about it yet. I'm still angry. I have to process what you've told me a bit before I can look at you face to face."

She listened to Malcolm's voice on the other end of the line.

"No, I actually I do really want to talk about it, I just need a little more time. How 'bout I see you back at the motel in two hours."

Malcolm spoke again and she made a sour face.

"No Mal. No, it's really important. I need to see you."

She let out a loud sigh.

"Malcolm, if you're not at our room in two hours you may not be married in the morning. You understand?"

Silence.

"Okay?"

Malcolm agreed.

"Okay then. See you soon."

Elle hung up the phone and went back to her test messages. She found the next address and punched it into the GPS, then pulled out of the driveway and headed back towards LSD. The address she entered was deep on the south side of the city.

Thirty-five minutes later she pulled her car up to the curb in front of a battered and dirty concrete box that served as low income housing. She reloaded the gun and hopped out of the car to head into the building. At the front door she found the entrance locked and a long panel of buzzer buttons next to the doors. She scanned through the buttons until she found what she was looking for.

307 - A. Logan.

The shallowest of grins spread across Elle's face, and she reached out and pressed 306.

The room lit up in an instant. It was harsh blue light and it cast unnatural shadows on the far walls and ceiling. The alarming light was accompanied by a harsh trill. Detective Upton sat up urgently in bed and grabbed his phone from his nightstand. He quickly swiped the answer button and climbed out of bed as quietly as he could.

"Who is calling you before sun-up?" his wife asked, sounding groggy and annoyed.

"I don't know honey. Go back to sleep," he said and stepped out of the bedroom and closed the door.

He glanced at the phone. It was a local number he didn't recognize.

"Hello?" he said, more as a question than a greeting.

"Detective Upton?" came the voice on the other end of the line.

"Yes. Who is this?"

"Detective, it's Malcolm Karma. I'm sorry if I woke you."

Upton wiped his face with the palm of his free hand and yawned.

"Mr. Karma, I'm not sure if I can arrest you for calling me on my personal cell, at home, at..." He paused and looked at the clock on the wall. "Three-thirty in the morning, but I assure you, I'm going to look into it."

"Detective," Malcolm said, without a smidge of humor in his voice. "I'm going to need you to take me seriously for just a little bit here. Okay?"

Upton walked into his kitchen and removed a coffee mug and jar of instant coffee from the cabinet next to the sink. Then he turned on the faucet as hot as it would go and let the water run until he started to see steam.

"What do you need Mr. Karma? What is so important that you called me at home, and as a matter of fact, how did you get this number in the first place?"

He scooped a heaping tablespoon of coffee crystals into the mug, then held it under the faucet.

"That's not really important," Malcolm said.

"It's important to me!" Upton shot back.

Malcolm sighed and the detective sipped his coffee.

"Detective, I know who blew up my apartment. I know who it is, where they are, and I know other things that they've done. Bigger things."

"Mr. Karma. I know who it was too. I'm talking to him right now."

Malcolm sighed again and Upton thought he could hear other voices in the background.

"Where are you Mr. Karma?"

"I'm in my car heading back to my motel. I think maybe you should meet me there."

"Mr. Karma, I need to tell you that if you are threatening or suggesting some kind of illegal act to me right now, that can be used against you in court."

"Yeah, that's fine," Malcolm said, in a distracted tone. "If you want to bring backup that might be a good idea too."

Upton took another sip of coffee and cleared his throat.

"Mr. Karma, what is it that's going to happen this morning?"

"I'm pretty sure some people are going to die Detective. I'm hoping you can make sure it's the right ones."

After that the phone went dead. Upton stared at the blank screen for a full minute trying to parse what just happened. He wasn't sure he understood it all, and he was even less sure he trusted anything that came out of Malcolm Karma's mouth. All of that said, Malcolm had just said that people were going to die, and as a police officer, hell as a person, he couldn't just ignore that.

He gulped down the rest of his coffee and walked back to his bedroom to get dressed. Malcolm had said to bring backup, but Upton wasn't about to risk his reputation on the force based on anything from Karma. No, he would go alone. He'd see what was what, and if needs be, he would call for reinforcements from the scene.

He threw on a clean-ish suit, grabbed his gun from the lock box in his closet and kissed his wife on the forehead. Then he walked out the front door of his house.

Chapter Twenty-Four

Mica presses the button for 307 and we wait. After a moment she presses it again, holding it down for a couple seconds. When nothing happens she sighs and runs her fingers through her hair.

"What now?" Allie asks.

"He's got to be home," Mica says, under her breath.

The two of them look at me as if expecting me to have a solution.

"Hey," I say. "I just a grunt. I don't do the thinking parts."

"Well, you're the muscle," Allie jabs. "Why don't you try and-"

The front door swings open and an elderly woman steps out and shoves her way past us. Mica reaches over and grabs the door as it's swinging closed.

"I figured it out," she says.

"You're a genius," I offer, flatly.

We file into the lobby and head up the stairs to the third floor. The place isn't bad. It's not a luxury condominium or anything, but it's clean and well lit. The walls are old and faded, but there's no graffiti or gang signs on them. I wonder, for a moment, if Alex picked this place because it was clean, or if it's clean because Alex Pilsen lives here.

When we reach 307 the door is open. Not all the way, just a crack, like the latch didn't catch when it swung shut.

"That doesn't seem good," Allie says.

Mica doesn't say anything, she just pushes the door gently and lets it swing open. The lights are off in the entryway, and living room, but there's a soft glow coming from a door half open on the other side of the space.

"Alex," Mica says, in a hesitant tone.

Nothing.

Allie and I stand just inside the doorway, cold sweat starting to drip down the back of my neck. Mica steps into the apartment and crosses the rug, past the sofa, to the source of the light. She pushes the door open and her face goes pale.

"Fuck," she says.

Allie and I cross the room quickly and look over her shoulder. Alex is naked, lying in the bath, blood splattered on the tile behind him. The water is still spraying out of the shower head, running down his face and carrying crimson out of the hole in his head, across the ceramic tub, and down the drain.

"Crap," I say.

"Do we call the cops?" I ask.

Both women look at me like I'm stupid.

"Then what?"

"Guns," Mica says. "We need to find his guns."

"Lovely," Allie groans.

"Fast," Mica says. "We don't have much time, we have to get out of the city and back to Malcolm's motel."

"Ya'll are a bundle of fun," Allie says.

The parking lot of the motel is full when we pull in. I look over at Allie and give a worried expression.

"I have a bad feeling about this," I say.

"You ain't just whistlin' Dixie," Allie says.

Mica is silent, which doesn't make me feel any better about the situation. I park the car opposite my room, over by the management offices with the bad coffee. We sit for a while in silence.

"What are we doin' Mal?" Allie says, staring straight out the windshield.

"We're sitting," I say.

She turns her head and looks at me, then turns back.

"I think Allie would like to know what we're doing next," Mica chimes in from the back seat.

I nod.

"I know what she meant. I just don't have an answer for her right now. Not yet."

We sit a little longer in silence, then a glint of light catches my eye from the rearview mirror. I glance up and see the door to my motel room standing open and my wife walking slowly across the mostly gravel parking lot towards my car.

She's dressed casually in jeans and a tight fitting t-shirt. She's beautiful and elegant and sways in a uniquely sexy way when she walks. I find myself forgetting, for a moment, what she's done and remembering why I love her. Then I notice the pistol in her right hand.

"We're gonna need to kill her," Mica says, softly.

I turn around in my seat and stare at her.

"What?"

"There's more of us than her, and we're all armed. We need to put her down now, before she gets to the car."

I feel a lump form in my throat. I swallow hard in an attempt to clear it.

"No, the killing needs to stop. We need to be the one's who stop it. We need to stop it now."

Mica nods sadly.

"Mal, there's going to be killing this morning. You said it yourself to Detective Upton. People are going to die here today. I'd rather it not be us."

"I'd rather that too," Allie says, quietly.

"Right," Mica says. "She's got a brunch."

I turn forward again and stare in the rearview mirror. Elle is almost halfway across the lot and her grip on the gun seems to have become more pronounced. The back door of the car swings open and Mica jumps out.

"Malcolm!" Allie shouts and I burst out of the car after her.

I stumble and race to grab Mica. Elle raises the weapon in her hand and I dive onto Mica's back, pulling her to the ground as a shot echos off the surrounding brick. There's a loud rumble and a hiss like steam bursting from a pipe and when we look up there's a Mack truck, sans the trailer, on the gravel between us and Elle.

The engine rumbles and dies and the doors swing open. On our side Ms. Erica, the nomadic bounty hunter staying in the room next to mine, steps out. I assume her partner Robin Hill must have been driving and is exiting the other side of the cab. Either way, Erica has a notably serious expression on her face and carries a handgun larger than anything I've ever seen.

"Everyone needs to settle down a little," comes Robin's voice, from the other side of the truck.

"This'll all be over soon," Erica says, pointing her piece at me and Mica.

Mica and I stand up and bush ourselves off.

"You should all probably put your guns down on the ground now," Erica says.

"You first," Mica says flatly.

I hear Robin chuckle.

"It's okay darlin'," she says. "We're all just waitin' on the boss. Until then, let's just take a deep breath."

At that moment a black BMW pulls into the motel and stops directly behind the semi.

"Oh fuck," Mica says.

"What?" I whisper.

The car's lights turn off and the engine stops. The driver side door opens and a striking brunette with features that appear to be drawn on her steps out of the car.

"My boss is here," Mica says.

Chapter Twenty-Five

Autumn stepped out of her sleek black BMW and strode around the semi cab, out of sight from Malcolm and Mica. There were no sounds, save for the soft crunch of gravel under her shoes. When she emerged at the nose of the truck she was accompanied by Elle and Robin.

The three of them approached the pair quietly wearing serious faces. Erica slammed the door of the truck and joined the posse creating a sort of lopsided diamond. Faraday at the front, dressed for all intents like she was preparing to argue a case before the Supreme Court. Over her suit was a long black wool coat with her hands stuffed deep in its pockets.

The rest of the group was spread out behind her. Elle to her left and Robin and Erica close to each other on her right. They closed in on Mal and Mica, stopping just past what would have been a comfortable distance.

The whole group stood in silence for a while. There was an uncomfortable sense that everyone was sizing each other up. Hands hovered nervously near pockets and waistbands. Nobody moved, nobody talked. Finally Faraday broke the silence.

"Well, we've all got ourselves in a bit of a predicament here, haven't we?"

S.A. Faraday stands in front of us, close enough to smell the coffee on her breath. I think about how coffee seems the wrong beverage for this moment. I know I could use a stiff drink. We're all nervous and it shows on everyone's faces. It's a stand off, and while we are easily outnumbered, it hardly matters when everyone has guns.

I grip the sawed off shotgun I borrowed from Alex's corpse, in my right hand. I'm fidgeting absentmindedly with the thin steel trigger. There's a Glock tucked in the front of my waistband and a Smith And Wesson in the back.

Mica is holding a Beretta nine mil' and I know she has another stashed somewhere on her body. The moment someone moves it'll be all over for everyone. We stand in this stalemate position for what feels like forever. I consider the option of speaking up.

I could offer to leave town, disappear. I could say I won't talk, I'll just vanish and everything can go back to the way it was, but of course it can't. That's what started this whole mess in the first place. All this because I wanted to leave.

"Well," Autumn says finally. "We've all got ourselves in a bit of a predicament here haven't we?"

The silence that follows answers the question precisely. I look at the stone faces of the group and let out a long sigh. I loosen my grip on the shotgun and let it slip before gripping it by its stubby barrel. I hold it out in front of me and slowly crouch down. The weapon goes silently onto the gravel in front of me and I stand back up with my hands stretched out in front of me. Very slowly I reach down to my waist with my right hand.

The group tenses and Elle and Erica point their weapons at my chest. The grip of the Glock meets my hand and I gently pull it out and drop it on the ground. I turn gradually, giving my wife and her crew my back and repeat the same action with the revolver. Then I turn back around and kick the guns on the ground away from me.

"Nothing has to happen here," I say. "I'm the cause of all this. I get it. I can disappear."

The words sound feeble and useless coming out of my mouth. I know that my offer is pointless. I know that it's not a viable solution, but I have nothing else to offer. I'm out of ideas.

"I'm as guilty of, well, everything, as anyone else here. You know I won't talk. I can just leave."

Elle huffs.

Faraday smiles coyly.

"That's not what I want," Faraday says. "That's not it at all, Malcolm."

I look at Mica who has a blank expression of panic on her face.

"Well," I say, hesitantly. "What is it that you do want?"

Elle takes a few steps forward, aligning herself with Faraday. She straightens up and a wild grin spreads across her face. She raises the barrel of her oversized silver revolver from my chest to my face. Her right thumb reaches up and pulls the heavy hammer back and a dull click cuts through the chilly dawn air as the hammer locks in place.

Faraday looks at me with an expression of thoughtfulness.

"Well Mal, to put it plainly, I want you."

"Dead."

That's what Elle expected The Faraday Woman to say next.

"I want you dead."

But it didn't come. There was just uncomfortable silence. She felt her smile falter and crack. There was an awful feeling in the pit of her stomach like when she rode in an elevator that moved too fast.

Malcolm looked confused too. His forehead wrinkled a bit and his eyebrows bunched up.

"You've done a great job Mal," The Faraday Woman said. "Mistakes have been made and we have some serious problems to overcome, but none of that is your fault."

Elle felt a numb tingle start to form in her back between her shoulder blades and her grip on the pistol in her hands tightened unconsciously. Her mouth was drying up and she had a lump in her throat. None of this was sounding like it was supposed to. This wasn't the fierce confrontation she had been expecting, rehearsing over and over in her head.

Mal shifted his weight from one foot to the other, but left his hands up, palms exposed. He was nervous too, as he should be. Wherever this strange speech was going, one thing was certain, it would be the last thing he ever heard.

"I don't think I'm following you," he said.

The Faraday Woman smiled.

"The Organization works Mal. On the whole it does what it's supposed to. It has a job, an important job, and it accomplishes it. We're having some management issues lately. We need to restructure."

Elle felt her face flush. This wasn't happening. She wasn't really going to let him live was she? Elle felt bile squirt up her throat. She wasn't going to move him up too? Make them partners? Elle had been living a nightmare for so long. Living with a man she didn't love. Letting this pathetic peon kiss her and fuck her. Tonight was supposed to end all that. She was supposed to finally be able to tell him how he made her stomach turn. She was supposed to get her revenge for all the years of humiliation. She couldn't keep doing it, she couldn't live with him any longer.

"Okay?" Mal said, hedging.

"So," The Faraday Woman continued. "I want you to step up. Be my guy. Clean out the rest of the deadwood and take over Mica's spot. I want you to run the city with me."

The shot was so loud it actually startled Elle. In retrospect she couldn't even remember turning the gun. It was all hazy and dreamlike, but the results were real. The Faraday Woman collapsed on the ground in a heap of silk, blood, and raw meat. Her head was gone and her body looked like a wet sack of potatoes just lying in the dirt.

Everyone's shouting. I hit the ground reflexively and there are long seconds before I regain the presence of mind to look around. There's gunfire coming from everywhere. Mica is lying on the ground behind me emptying the magazine on the second of her weapons, the first already cleaned out and tossed aside. Faraday is piled up on the ground looking like nothing more than a bundle of blood soaked rags, and Elle is next to her blowing blood bubbles from her lips and nostrils. She has two entry wounds in her back and a hole in her neck that's spurting crimson in a rhythmic pattern.

The ladies are farther back. Robin is on the ground choking, and Ms. Erica is pulling the trigger over and over again on a, now, empty pistol while trying to drag her partner back to the truck.

The gunfire stops, but there's still shouting. Mica screaming at me to get back to the car. I hear Allie cursing and telling us both to move. Elle is wheezing, coughing and whispering for me to help her. Ms. Erica is sobbing wildly and still, uselessly, pulling the trigger on her gun. The hum of an engine fades into the foreground and the crackle of new tires on gravel fills the air.

Chapter Twenty-Six

The handcuffs hurt more than I expected them to. I'm in a small cell, a holding cell of some kind I expect. It's about eight by ten with some kind of reinforced chain link wire across the front instead of bars. The walls on the other three sides are cinderblock, painted a dull off white. There are low stainless steel benches along the two side walls and a payphone with a comically short, six inch cord between the box and the receiver.

I've been here about an hour and no one has come to check on me. I don't know who else they have, or for that matter who else is alive after the massacre at the motel. Faraday was dead for sure. Her head was blown all the way off by Elle when she offered me Mica's job.

That was a surprise. I did not see that coming. Neither did Elle, from her reaction. I suppose she thought she was in line for that spot. The truth is, I doubt Faraday wanted me either. She probably was just trying to stall for time, or maybe get me to turn on Mica and Allie. Either way, I'm pretty sure she meant to kill us all in the end.

Elle was still alive when Upton ratcheted the cuffs on

me. She was spitting up blood and her eyes were starting to get that far away look, but she was alive. I have no idea if that remains true.

Mica was alive and, as far as I could tell, uninjured. She was in retreat, still packing heat and spitting distance from the car. I hadn't seen Allie since I got out of the car, and her calls for us to bolt stopped as soon as the cops hit the scene. I hope she ran. I hope she got out clean and makes for Canada, or Mexico, or Europe.

I'm pretty sure Robin was dead. She was limp in her partner's arms as she sat pulling that damn trigger, sobbing and choking on her own tears. I have no doubt that Erica is in custody, she didn't seem able to move, let alone run.

All of that is just speculation though. I haven't seen anyone since Detective Upton and his crew swarmed the scene. I was already face down on the ground, it was easy for him to take me away, which is fine because I wouldn't have run anyway. I'm tired. I'm tired of the hiding, of the secrets, and of the running. I'm tired of not having a real life. I'm tired of the killing.

I'm going to go to prison. I know that. I'm going to get locked away for a very long time, and I have to say that, surprisingly, I'm looking forward to it. Prison isn't safe, but it's predictable and right now that's what I crave. Simplicity and predictability. I'm sure I can trade some information for some kind of protective custody agreement, and then I can just live out the rest of my life in peace. That's what I crave most now. Just peace.

"Karma, on your feet shithead."

Finally, someone coming. I'm eager to get the process moving. I jump to my feet and step up to the wire wall.

"Yes officer, what can I do for you?"

"Shut your pie hole for starters. You've got a lot of

jabbering to do in the next few weeks, you don't need to waste the air with me."

I nod.

"You've got people here to see you."

"People?" I ask.

"Shut up," the cop says.

The door to the cell slides open and the cop takes me by the arm. He walks me down a long narrow hallway made of the same featureless blocks that the cell was built from. At the end of the hall is a metal door painted tuxedo blue. The cop sticks a long key in the door and turns it clockwise. He twists the knob and it swings open.

"In ya go," he says, and unlocks my cuffs from my wrists.

I get a little shove and the door slams behind me.

The room is only slightly larger than the cell I was just in. It's all cinder block painted the same baby blue as the door, which it turns out, is still better than the drab off white of the cell. There's no mirror or window, this isn't an interrogation room. It's a private space. It's a place for suspects to consult with their lawyers, which is why mine is sitting at the small gray metal table in the middle of the room.

"Malcolm," Allie says.

My face goes pale, I can feel the blood rush out of my skin. A new lump materializes in my throat and I audibly choke on it. I cough and sputter and my body goes cold.

"Allie, what are you-"

She puts a finger to her lips and mimes the shush sound.

"I came as soon as I heard," she says with fire in her eyes.

I nod and her serious expression melts away to a friendly smile.

"It seems you've gotten yourself into a predicament Mr. Karma."

I nod again, still feeling lost and confused.

"From what I can gather," she goes on. "It appears to me to be a bit of a wrong place at the wrong time situation. Am I right?"

"You could say that," I stammer.

"Still, I imagine you know things. Things you might not even know you know."

I give a hesitant shrug and she mimes that I should speak out loud.

"I don't know," I say. "How would I know what I don't know I know?"

"Good point," she says cheerfully. "That's why you have me. Your wife was into some bad stuff Mal. I'm sure you had no idea, but it's possible that you could have some knowledge that could clear up some questions."

"I...don't really see how," I say.

"I'm sure you don't now, but we'll figure it out. The cops, they think that this was all you. Apparently there was a secret safe in your old apartment, and well, that woman that your wife killed at the motel, she was the Cook County State's Attorney. I know you couldn't be involved, but you might have heard something over the years with Elle that could be helpful in proving it. I've made some calls and there's someone here that has some questions."

I look back confused.

Allie mouths the words 'trust me'.

I nod.

The door to the room opens and a man in his mid fifties walks in. He isn't a cop, that's for sure. He's well dressed in a dark suit. He's got black hair with just a little gray at the temples. He walks with confidence and composure. He steps up to me and puts out a hand.

"Mr. Karma," he says, with a deep strong voice. "I'm Special Agent Kyle Flannery. I'm with the F.B.I. I'd like to talk to you about S.A. Faraday and her relationship with your wife."

The door closes behind him.

As soon as the sound of the lock sliding into place echos through the room Agent Flannery's demeanor changes.

"Malcolm," he says, in a friendly but urgent tone. "Here's where things stand."

He takes a seat next to Allie and leans in close.

"Mica's gone. We're not sure where, but they don't have her in custody."

I look at Allie knowing that she was in the car and that Mica was heading that way. She looks back at me with steely eyes and flat lips.

"The woman going by Robin Hill is dead. She was DOA when Detective Upton got there. Her partner Erica Lynn is in custody, but they don't really have anything on her. She's not connected on paper anywhere to Faraday or Mica and they look like a couple of truckers that just drove into a bad situation. That's the story Ms. Lynn is giving to the police too. I don't think the local PD is going to be able to hold her for very long."

I nod.

"But the truth is they are, or were, mercenaries that State's Attorney Faraday used for ops she didn't trust Mica to take care of. They're the ones that blew up your building."

I frown.

"How did they get the bomb in there. I'm pretty sure I would have noticed someone breaking into my place."

Flannery nods.

"No, they didn't plant it. That was your wife."

I rub my face and let out a long sigh.

"And when did that happen?"

Flannery shrugs.

"No idea, but I imagine early on. Probably right after you moved in. She was a plant from the beginning. It was her job to keep an eye on you. Almost everyone in Faraday's organization had some kind of supervisor watching them."

I slump in my chair feeling exhausted.

"So, Mica's gone, Faraday's dead, her goons are dead or in custody for now. What about Elle? Where is she? Is she alive?"

Flannery and Allie exchange a glance.

"Elle's dead," Allie says flatly.

Flannery shifts in his seat.

"Malcolm, I think we need to start fresh. You're caught up as much as you need to be. Now we need to talk about going forward."

I sigh and straighten up in my chair.

"Yeah, honestly, I don't know how much help I'm going to be. I can speak to my actions and directives from Mica, but I don't really know anything else."

Flannery is staring at me slightly annoyed.

"I didn't even know Elle was involved until tonight, eh, last night now I guess. Anyway, I didn't know about Faraday, or Elle, or any of that. I don't think my testimony will be useful."

Flannery frowns and leans forward in his seat.

"Malcolm-"

"I haven't told him yet," Allie says.

Flannery looks at her with an expression of shock.

"I didn't have time," she says. "You got here faster than I expected."

"Malcolm," Flannery says without an ounce of friendliness. "I don't need your testimony. I need you. I need you to vanish. I need you to disappear."

It's like a bucket of cold water is dumped over me.

"What?" I say.

"Malcolm, this investigation has been going on a lot longer than you know. You're not the one we're after. Even Faraday was just a stepping stone for us. We're after the organization as a whole."

I frown and look at Allie. She stares back expressionless.

"I don't understand," I say. "It's over. Faraday was Mica's boss. She was the one running the show, and she's dead. Mica's gone you said, and without Faraday looming over her, I imagine she'll stay gone. It's over, it's finally over. I'm going to prison, and everyone else goes free."

Flannery Chuckles.

"No, Malcolm. It's not over. It's far from over. Faraday wasn't the boss any more than Mica. This goes a little higher than a county S.A. This goes well beyond that. We have a lot of work to do and I'm going to need your help, but you can't help me from behind bars, so, you're going to have to disappear."

A chill runs down my spine.

"I don't understand what you're saying."

"I'm afraid Malcolm, that your work is not done."

It took four hours for Flannery to get the papers transferring me to F.B.I. custody. I was cuffed again and walked out of the station by Flannery and another agent who never bothered to introduce himself. We're sitting in the back of a black SUV now, heading east on the Eisenhower expressway. I'm un-cuffed and sitting unrestrained, save for the seat belt. Flannery's been quiet for most of the drive. The other agent is in the front passenger seat and a third unknown man is driving the car.

At Lakeshore Drive we go south and exit again at Cermak. A little while later we stop. The building next to us is nondescript. It's brick and block and wears years of neglect. There's a green door on the corner and a worn yellow awning above it. It's definitely not an F.B.I. building. I feel my stomach turn.

The second agent, the one in the front passenger seat gets out of the truck. He walks across the street and climbs in a black sedan and drives away. I turn to Flannery who hasn't said anything since we pulled away from the police station.

"Where are we?" I ask.

Flannery looks at me seriously.

"Your new home," he says.

I choke.

"I'm sorry, you want me to live here?"

"It's better than prison isn't it?"

I look out the window at the crumbling building in a deserted neighborhood.

"Honestly," I say. "I'm not sure that's true."

"It was good enough for me," comes a voice from the driver's seat.

I turn and look at the man who's been driving silently since the suburbs. I squint. He's not old, but he's definitely past his thirties. It strikes me that he's not dressed like the other agents. He's in a suit, but less formal, less business. It's all black with a white shirt. It's my uniform. It's how I dressed when I worked for Mica.

I feel cold sweat pressing out my pores.

"And who are you?" I ask, suddenly knowing the answer.

The man unbuckles his seat belt and turns around to face me. He's handsome, chiseled, and frightening. He extends a hand between the front seats for me to shake. I reach out and grasp it and he squeezes me firmly.

"Sorry," he says. "Malcolm, my name is Gavin. Gavin Gayle. It's very nice to meet you."

The End

About the Author

 Neil Christiansen, author of Dark White and Malcolm Karma: Cold Turkey, has a unique blend of experiences in the world of theater and audio visual production management. His journey from the stage to the world of literature is a testament to his creativity and versatility.

Neil pursued a degree in theater. This academic background instilled in him a deep appreciation for storytelling and the arts, which would later find expression in his writing.

Neil is a proud parent of six children. For Neil, family is the cornerstone of his life, shaping his values and driving his creative endeavors.

Malcolm Karma started as a Twitter thread back in 2017, an attempt to overcome writer's block. It grew in popularity on the site, gaining readership before moving off of twitter and into a manuscript. Enjoy this new expansion into the universe of Gavin Gayle.